I0654717

Edward Hooker

Diary of Edward Hooker, 1805-1808

Edward Hooker

Diary of Edward Hooker, 1805-1808

ISBN/EAN: 9783337021054

Printed in Europe, USA, Canada, Australia, Japan

Cover: Foto ©Raphael Reischuk / pixelio.de

More available books at **www.hansebooks.com**

AMERICAN HISTORICAL ASSOCIATION.

DIARY OF EDWARD HOOKER, 1805-1808.

———

(From the Report of the Historical Manuscripts Commission of the American Historical Association for 1896, pages 842-929.)

WASHINGTON:
GOVERNMENT PRINTING OFFICE.
1897.

Edward Hooker, the writer of this diary, was born at Farmington, Conn., April 27, 1785.[1] He was the youngest child of Col. Noadiah Hooker, a Revolutionary officer, and a direct descendant in the fifth generation from the Rev. Thomas Hooker, the first minister of the First Church at Hartford, celebrated for his share in the founding of the colony of Connecticut. Edward Hooker was descended from Thomas Hooker's son, the Rev. Samuel Hooker, who was settled over the Congregational Church in Farmington in 1660, and died there in 1697, after a pastorate of thirty-seven years. Our diarist was graduated at Yale College in 1805, and immediately went to Columbia, S. C., where his elder brother, John Hooker, was engaged in the successful practice of law. It was Edward Hooker's intention to study law with his brother and to settle in the South. After a period of teaching in the academy at Cambridge, S. C., he was invited to a tutorship in the South Carolina College at Columbia, which he accepted, pursuing at the same time his legal studies with his brother. After about two years he accepted an invitation to a tutorship in Yale College, in which he spent about three years. In the spring of 1812 he was married to Elizabeth Daggett, a daughter of Henry Daggett, a merchant and prominent citizen of New Haven. He then, yielding to the urgent request of his parents, gave up the profession of the law, and settled down in Farmington to take care of them, and to manage their estate. The rest of his life was spent in the management of this farm. For a few years he prepared boys for college. He died May 15, 1846. He was for many years a deacon in the Congregational Church at Farmington, and was marked by public spirit and philanthropy. He left three children—one daughter, Eliza, who became the wife of the Hon. Francis Gillette of Hartford, United States Senator from Connecticut; and two sons, John Hooker, a lawyer at Hartford, who married Isabella, the daughter of Rev. Lyman Beecher; and Commander

[1] For the following facts relating to his life the editor is indebted to his son, John Hooker, esq., of Hartford. Conn.

Edward Hooker, **United States Navy**, retired, now living in Brooklyn, N. Y.

For many years it was Mr. Hooker's habit to keep a detailed journal or diary. The series originally consisted of twenty-eight paper-covered books, about 8½ by 7 inches, each consisting of about forty-eight pages. These were written, apparently daily, in a fine hand. Nos. 1, 2, and 3 were copied into two thicker and more substantial volumes, with some amplification of phrases, but, it would seem, with little if any other change. The series now, therefore, contains no No. 3. It begins with Commencement Day, September 11, 1805, and with the writer's graduation in a class which included Thomas H. Gallaudet, the founder of deaf-mute instruction in America; Heman Humphrey, afterwards president of Amherst College; and Gardiner Spring. Not long after, October 19, the young graduate set sail for Charleston. S. C., and proceeded thence to Columbia. The record of his experiences in the South, chiefly in South Carolina, during a period of three years, is to be found in Nos. 1, 2, 4, 5, 6, 7, 8, and 9 of this journal, and the following extracts are made from these volumes. For permission to copy and to use these extracts, the Commission is indebted to the kindness of John Hooker, esq., of Hartford, Conn., the son of the diarist.

As only a body of extracts from this voluminous diary could be presented, the editor has felt obliged, with much regret, to omit almost entirely the highly interesting portions which exhibit, in minute detail and apparently with much fidelity, the social life of South Carolina in these years. It seemed to him that, while every good picture of Southern life and manners is of value to historical students, there is a greater abundance of such portraiture than of printed documents illustrating the political history of South Carolina during the period in question. These three years are a part of a period of transition, during which the State was developing from the Federalist South Carolina of 1788 into the better known South Carolina of 1832. The process is one of extraordinary interest, and might well receive far more attention than has hitherto been bestowed upon it.

Not too much illumination of South Carolina history must be expected from the journal of a boy of 20 or 23. Not only was Hooker youthful, but he was prone to look at things and men from the special point of view of the old-fashioned college tutor, prone to overestimate the importance of the minutiæ of pronunciation, excessively interested in rhetoric and gesture. He had some measure, too, of New England censoriousness. Yet on the whole he is a candid and an intelligent observer. His mind was more mature than is usual at his age. He was of a social and affectionate nature, which inclined him before long to take a genial view of characters and customs which at first were strange to his grave and somewhat formal mind. But that which perhaps will most recommend his narrative as interesting to the modern reader is the opportunity which his residence at Columbia gave him to observe the external course of South Carolina politics and legislation at the capital of the State. It is not known to the editor that just such a picture of men and affairs at the State-house during those three years is elsewhere accessible. Especial attention should be called to the record of debates on the slave trade.

The diarist's description of Charleston and Beaufort and their society has been omitted, though with much regret, from a conviction that other descriptions of these things are, after all, obtainable. In the main, the extracts relate to days passed at Columbia. The most extensive exceptions to this statement occur in the case of a short tour in the mountainous parts of South Carolina and in the case of that portion of the final homeward journey in which Mr. Hooker writes of Raleigh, Richmond, Mount Vernon, and Washington.

J. FRANKLIN JAMESON.

EXTRACTS FROM THE DIARY.

[Mr. Hooker rode up from Charleston to Columbia with Col. Wade Hampton.]

November 4th, [1805]. * * * Crossing,[1] I entered the district of Richland of which the shire town, (and probably the only town in it) is Columbia.[2] Caesar[3] pointed out to me the State House which was just visible through the trees, about two miles forward. I was pleased with the hope of soon finishing my journey; but yet did not feel in very high spirits. A thousand anxious thoughts crowded into my mind. I could

---

[1] The Congaree River.
[2] Founded as a new capital in 1790. Columbia had now about 500 white inhabitants.
[3] Servant of Colonel Hampton, with whom the journey from Charleston had been made.

not avoid reflecting on my past situation, views and schemes, and the change which might be made in the future prospects and events of my life, by the simple determination to come into this region,—a change perhaps for the better,—perhaps for the worse. However I had not time to indulge very long in my reverie, before I found the woods breaking away on both sides, and an entirely new scene opening upon my view. A neat, handsome little town, on an elevated tract of ground, commanding on the west and south a view of 8 or 10 miles, and shrouded on the east and north by immense forests of pine. On coming up the hills of sand from Granby, I found myself at the head of Richardson Street, which is the principal one in the town, running north and south. To me however, it appeared to run east and west, and I was totally unable to realize that I was coming in on the south, and not on the east. I drove to Mr. Chapman's boarding house (opposite the State house) where brother J.[1] on his departure for the circuit, had made arrangements for my accommodation;   *   *   *

*   *   * About sunset the Governor of the State,[2] with his suite arrived in town from the Upper Country. They are dressed in military uniform, and make a gay appearance. He is out on a military tour; being required by the laws, to be present, with the Adjutant General, at all the regimental reviews. The Adjutant General has about 1200 dollars, and each of the Brigade Inspectors about 220 dollars a year for their services.   *   *   *

[*Nov. 5.*]   *   *   * Col. Hampton[3] called on me just before dinner, and invited me to come down some time before long, and make him a visit at his seat, a few miles below Columbia. Mr. Hammond[4] also called on me, and brought with him Mr. Hanford another of the Tutors of College.

Col. Hampton, I find, is considered by every body about here a very singular man:—one of a million. The leading traits of his character are boldness and originality of scheme, remarkable foresight in the judicious selection of means for the accomplishment of this scheme, and undaunted perseverance

[1] John Hooker, Yale College 1796, elder brother of Edward, now a lawyer in Columbia. See O'Neall, Bench and Bar of South Carolina, II, 247, 248.

[2] Paul Hamilton, governor of South Carolina 1804–1806, Secretary of the Navy 1809–1813.

[3] Col. Wade Hampton (1754–1835), M. C. 1795–1797, 1803–1805, afterwards noted as a general in the war of 1812; grandfather of the Gen. Wade Hampton of the civil war.

[4] Presumably Elisha Hammond (Dartmouth, 1802), who for a brief period was professor of languages in the college, and who was the father of Governor and Senator James H. Hammond.

in the application of these means. In his conversations with me, during our journey, he had a great deal to say about energy of character, and enterprize: and well he might: for he himself furnishes a striking lesson of what may be effected by such a spirit;—having by means of it, risen to an eminence in property, station and information that astonishes every one who knows the small beginnings with which he started on the career of active life. He was born in Virginia: His father's family was large and without much property: so that the Colonel with his brothers, was brought up to labor in the field; and was almost entirely without the advantages of even a common school education. By the time he was thirty years old, or before, he commanded an intrepid regiment of cavalry, that distinguished itself at the battle of Eutaw Springs,[1] and performed various other important services during the revolution. Some time after the war, he was for several years high sheriff of the large District of Camden, including several counties. Since then he has been two or three times elected a member of Congress. By various ways, some honest, and some, it is said, dishonest he has acquired an immense estate in land and negroes, which, if report be true, yields him an annual income of more than Fifty thousand dollars. He seems to have availed himself of every opportunity to acquire knowledge: and is able to converse with ease and spirit, on most subjects that are agitated in most companies. His acquaintance with good authors is very considerable: but he seems to have mostly read those who are characterized by justness of thought, rather than by beauty of language. His language is more than ordinarily pure, forcible, clear and concise,—and he is said to have acquired it, much more by strict attention to the conversation and writings of well educated men, than to the study of grammatical and rhetorical rules. In his conversation, he sometimes in the midst of a sentence, hesitates for a word; but to one who is acquainted with him, this produces no unpleasant sensation; a perfect confidence being felt, that the word, whenever it does come, will compensate, by its peculiar aptness, for all the delay which it has occasioned. For the tinsel of language he entertains a sovereign contempt;—and he has no mercy upon those who speak in a harmonious, studied style without good sense: Indeed he is disposed, he says, to consider style as of very inferior, or no importance. He calls Mr. Elliott

[1] September 8, 1781.

of Vermont a speaker of the above description, and thinks him, literally, an impertinent fool. Dr. Eustis he thinks a very sensible and handsome speaker. Mr. R. Griswold, he speaks highly of, and considers him one of the first rate speakers.

As a man, Col. Hampton has some qualities that interest us, but I should think him deficient in that tender and amiable sensibility, which, more than anything else, makes us love our fellow creatures. People relate some things about his dealings with his brothers, which though not uncommon, in the case of worldly men, who are without any ties of consanguinity or affection, are, in the case of brothers, to say the least, very unkind. However, some of his brothers' children have experienced from him considerable liberality. In his politics, he is, I hardly know what. He appears to set very little value on names, and to discover very little of that prejudiced feeling, which, now a days, is so apt to accompany the mention of any particular denomination of parties. He is called a republican: yet he certainly has many notions and sentiments which are more characteristic of federalism. And he does not hesitate to condemn, openly, and unequivocally some measures of the republican party. I have heard related an anecdote, which strikingly exhibits his wish to be candid, and his indignation at the prevailing practice of blending every interest in society with party politics, and forcing everything to bend to what is called "republicanism" or "federalism" according as these or those political opinions happen to predominate in any section of the country. The Board of Trustees to the State College recently established in this town,[4] had occasion last year to make an appointment to the Presidency of the institution. The two candidates most talked of were President Maxcy of Rhode Island[5] and the Rev. Dr. M'Calla of the low country.[6] Several of the Trustees were violent partizans: and among

---

[1] James Elliott (1770-1839), a Federalist Member of Congress from Vermont 1803-1809.

[2] Dr. William Eustis (1753-1825), Member of Congress 1801-1805, 1820-1823, Secretary of War 1807-1813, governor of Massachusetts 1823-1825.

[3] Roger Griswold of Connecticut (1762-1812). Member of Congress 1795-1805, governor of Connecticut 1811-1812.

[4] The College of South Carolina, chartered December 19, 1801, in which Mr. Hooker was subsequently a tutor.

[5] Jonathan Maxcy (1768-1820), acting president of Rhode Island College (now Brown University) 1792-1797, president 1797-1802, president of Union College 1802-1804, of the South Carolina College 1804-1820. Life by Romeo Elton.

[6] Dr. Daniel McCalla (1748-1809) who from 1788 until his death was pastor of the Congregational Church at Wappetaw, S. C. Life by Hollingshead.

the rest Chancellor James;[1] who, just before the election came on, met Col. Hampton in the street, and began the following conversation.—" Well Colonel, have you made up your mind yet? *Col. H.* I have thought over the subject considerably; but I am still open to conviction. *Chancellor.* Well sir, I'll tell you what 'tis. We must have a republican at the head of our College, or all is lost: We would a great deal better have done nothing about it. *Colonel.* Indeed, this is presenting the subject in a new point of view. I had not myself considered it in this light before. But are you sure that your man is one of this description? *Chancellor.* Dr. M'Calla is, I am sure, a man that can be depended on—a man of known—of tried republicanism. He isn't one of your still sort;—afraid to speak his sentiments; but he comes out boldly and takes a decided part on our side of politics. I am sure you'll think it better to take him than to send away to New England for a man whom we don't know. *Colonel.* But are you sure that Dr. M'Calla is a republican—Are you sure that he can be depended on? *Chancellor.* Yes. I have it from the best authority, that he is a staunch Jeffersonian republican. *Colonel.* Then, sir, depend upon it, he does not have my vote. I want none of your staunch republicans at the head of our college:—nor your staunch Federalists neither. Our object is of a totally different nature. I know of no necessary connection between party politics and literature; and till a candidate presents some better recommendation for the office than staunch republicanism I shall employ my influence to keep him out of it." On the subject of the tendency of our political institutions, Col. Hampton told me he was inclined to think, the fears of leading characters in the northern States, such as Gov. Strong, Gov. Treadwell, Mr. Tracy, Dr. Dwight[2] and the clergy in general, that the turbulent spirit of the people might lead to licentiousness, were not without foundation:—that he himself had also thought it might affect and weaken the government;—but then he believed there was more of the turbulent, licentious, fractious spirit in the common people of the northern States than of the southern. He mentioned his tour to the north a few years since, and the incivilities he

[1] William D. James, a chancellor of the Court of Equity from 1802 to 1824, and a judge of the Court of Appeals from 1824 to 1828. O'Neall, Bench and Bar of South Carolina, I, 236-240.

[2] Caleb Strong, at this time governor of Massachusetts. John Treadwell, at this time lieutenant governor, afterwards governor of Connecticut. Uriah Tracy, Senator from Connecticut. Timothy Dwight, president of Yale College from 1795 to 1817.

met with from the low bred people. He thought there was more
civility to strangers, to gentlemen riding in their carriages,
more submission to the laws, and respect of authority in the
south.—In his religious opinions, the Colonel is thought to be
rather loose: Indeed he has sometimes, rather in pleasantry,
when asked about his creed, called himself "a loose christian."—
Our conversation, while on the road last Sunday morning,
turning on religion, the Colonel told me he did not believe there
was a tenth part of the number of deists in this State that
there is in Connecticut : for that rigidness and illiberality on the
subject which prevails there disgusts many with the Christian
system. As for himself, he said he only wished to come in, like
the rest, for his share, in the general dispensation of God's
blessings, such as an ordinary share of health, the use of the
earth, the seasons &c. but he should never ask any particular
blessings and favors; for he did not suppose that would make
any difference about obtaining them:—if it would, says he,
the system of Gods dealing with men would be a system of
favoritism.—This "powowing" says he, may be of some use to
the individual : it may preserve in him a humble spirit that
will help to keep his passions subdued; and thus be of real
service : but it can have no other effect. He believed that we
are just what our Creator designed us to be, and not that man
had fallen from his original state of goodness, and thus disappointed the Deity and thwarted his designs. Of course, what
Moses says about man's fall and the doctrine of original sin, he
believed to be a vile fabrication. He should not puzzle himself about the intricacies of theology, for he was fixed on certain principles, and he trusted himself to his maker for the
result of the matter. He believed in a future state of rewards
and punishments.

Possibly, however, the Colonel was not sincere in all this,
for finding that I very much disagreed with him on the subject, he afterwards told one of the officers of the college that I
belonged to the "true school" for he had sounded me, on the
road, as we were travelling together.

As to his moral conduct, it appears to be, and it is said to be
outwardly correct, so far as it respects the prevailing vices of
the country. He does not get drunk;—he despises gambling
as a mean and pernicious employment;—he speaks with much
abhorrence of the prevailing lasciviousness of the young. He
is however accused of great frauds in land speculation, and of

violating a law of the State which existed a few years ago, by privately bringing in negro slaves from North Carolina.

One of the principal maxims of Col. Hampton's life and which he strongly recommended to me has been to *Consider everything certain which is possible.* He thinks it an all-important maxim for a young man to adopt, when setting out in the world, and one, which, if steadily adhered to, will make the common discouragements of life dwindle into insignificance, and enable him to do wonders in his day.—He despises noticing little complaints of body or trifles of any kind,—and believes that diseases are often produced merely by giving way to small indispositions. When diseases of a really serious nature are about to attack one, they are preceded by certain symptoms; these symptoms may be easily known, and should be early attended to.

On our journey we had considerable conversation about the different systems of settlement that prevail in the Northern and Southern States. The Colonel is very fond of retired life—that is, a retired life in the strictest sense of the word. He wishes to be two or three miles at least from any neighbors. He utterly disapproves of the custom of farmers in Connecticut who for the sake of society, cluster together into villages and hamlets, instead of setting their habitations in the midst of their lands, where they can manage them to the greatest advantage. He thinks the tendency of these village settlements is to make people more contracted, less hospitable and less friendly. If he has a friend, he says he don't want him to be a near neighbor: he should be sure to lose his friendship; for there would be some difficulty about fences, damages, things borrowed, or something to disturb harmony.

Colonel H's personal appearance is not very striking. Stature not over middling. Dresses in good clothes, but has nothing showy about him. A great enemy to finery, and treats it with marked contempt. There is nothing commanding or peculiarly dignified in his appearance; though he has an easy and becoming dignity of manners. He appears to much the best advantage when mounted; being an unusually expert horseman. When standing, and especially if engaged in conversation, he is very apt to rest on one leg, and to throw out the other so far as to give him a stooping posture; while at the same time his arms are placed *akimbo*, and his eyes cast on the ground.

November 6th. (Wednesday) This forenoon, I called on Mr.
Hanford, and with him took a view of the college buildings
which are erecting, on a pleasant rise of ground about ¼ of a
mile southeast of the State House.   The place though so near
the center of the town is however very recluse; there being no
houses around, and even the lands being uncleared and covered
with lofty pines, and wild shrubs.   The plan is to have two
buildings of perhaps 160 feet in length each, facing each other
at the distance of 160 feet apart.   At right angles to these,
and facing the area inclosed between them, it is proposed to
place the President's house; and afterwards, as occasion may
require, other buildings, such as the dining hall and professors
houses are expected to be built fronting each other, and rang-
ing in a line with the first mentioned long buildings.   The
buildings A and B are erected, and A is finished except the

central part, which is however
advanced so far as to be capable
of use.   The central parts are designed for the Chapel, Library,
Philosophical Chamber, Recita-
tion Rooms, &c.—the wings are
designed for scholars' mansion
rooms—C is the site of the President's house, D the place for a dining hall, E for a Professor's house
perhaps.   That part of the work

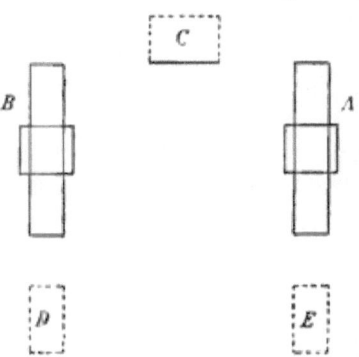

which is done is in a handsome, though not all in a durable stile.
The chapel occupies the two lower stories of the central building on the right, and is in a beautiful style of workmanship both
within and without.   The Library room above is supported by
four stately Tuscan columns, which rise from the area of the
chapel with considerable majesty, and give to the room an
appearance of grandeur.   The galleries are supported by a
row of smaller pillars.   The room is nearly or quite square.
The pulpit is surrounded by a semi-octagonal stage, on the
right and left sides of which are steps leading to the officers'
seats and thence are other steps to the pulpit.   The upper
tiers of windows are semi-circular at top, as in Episcopal
churches and have some neat ornamental work about them.
The stage, pulpit, staircases, bannisters, seats, &c. are all
painted white, and make, now, a very chaste and pretty appearance; but I question if they will long remain so.   There are

but a few seats, and these are so arranged near the outside of the room, as to leave a large area in the centre, on the sides and in front of the stage. The wings are three stories high, and are divided into 12 mansion rooms each, and 24 bedrooms. The bedrooms are directly back of the large rooms; and the arrangement is such as to be very convenient for ventilation— a circumstance very necessary to be attended to in this warm climate.

The munificence of the legislature towards this institution has been very honorable. They first granted 50,000 dollars out of the public treasury for the two long buildings. They have granted several thousands for books and instruments, and they are to appropriate a considerable sum annually for its constant support.[1] The College was opened for the reception of students some months ago. The number, I believe, is about 30. They board together with the tutors at a private house. * * *

Saturday Nov. 9th. * * * P. M. Walked up to the College about 4 o'clock, and visited the Library with Mr. Hammond. The room is very spacious, airy and handsome. About 5000 volumes have been purchased but not more than 3000 have yet arrived. Many of these have an elegant appearance; but it is thought the selection was not made very judiciously. It was made by a Committee of gentlemen in Charleston; of whom Judge Johnson[2] of the Federal Court was a principal one. There seems to be an undue proportion of modern works— many of them of the ephemeral class. There are large piles of periodical works, such as the Gentleman's Magazine, European Magazine, Annual Register, and others of no more solid worth than these. Some handsome editions of the Greek and Latin Classics and translations—A few books written in the Oriental languages. * * *

Nov. 10th. (Sunday). * * * There are no meetings regularly held here on the Sabbath except by the Methodists. They are peculiarly engaged on the subject of religion, and, I find, give considerable displeasure to some of the Columbians by their noisy zeal. At evening, Mr. Egan[3] and Dr. Brazier called

---

[1] Reports bound with the Acts of 1807 show an annual appropriation of $6,000 by the legislature, besides expenditures of $8,000 on the president's house and $4,400 for other purposes. In 1805 1806, $11,390 were paid out for the college.

[2] William Johnson, associate justice of the Supreme Court of the United States 1804–1834.

[3] Thomas Henry Egan, law partner of John Hooker. See O'Neall, Bench and Bar of South Carolina, II. 231, 232.

on me; and with Miss Mary-Ann Chapman[*] we attended one
of their meetings. The order of the exercises did not differ
much from that of Congregational meetings. The singing
was much better than I expected it would be. The lines were
read by the preacher and sung by the audience alternately.
Most and perhaps all the singers sung the same part. If
there was any bass, it was so small as to be overwhelmed by
the burst of melodious sounds from the men, and women, in the
gallery and below, promiscuously engaged in the same part.
This was something new to me. It struck my fancy very much,
and made a most agreeable impression. From the account
which has been given me of Methodist meetings, I had expected
to witness more indecorum, and irregularity. Some groans
were made; though I did not think they were very natural
ones. The preaching did not entirely please me. A great part
of the sermon was certainly bordering on extravagance. I
was glad to see the preacher warm, as every preacher should
be; but I was sorry to see his warmth not in the least tempered
by judgment. Whether repeating the text, quoting scripture,
stating the heads of his discourse reasoning, or addressing the
passions, it was all one uninterrupted current of affected pathos
and monotonous roar. Even between the different heads of
discourse, he had no more stop or intermission of voice than
between connected sentences—nor between different sentences
had he hardly any thing more than common pauses. There
was a closing prayer by another preacher (a Mr. Moore) which
was excellent and well delivered. The audience appeared well
dressed and respectable. I saw nothing like levity exhibited
by any body present. The house was filled with people. All
those who were in the gallery were blacks. The inhabitants
speak highly of the Rev. Mr. Dunlap, an ordained Presbyterian
minister of this place who died summer before last. He was
an able and good man;—and was educated at Winnsborough
Academy or College (as it is called) a little seminary about 30
miles north. He depended on no contract, but voluntary con-
tribution for his support, which for the first two or three years
was liberal, but gradually died away; so that he at length left
preaching and taught an academy. He was also appointed
Clerk of the Senate, and from the emoluments of that office
derived a good subsistence.

  Monday Nov. 11th. The township of Columbia is not large;
being only two miles square. This territory is laid out into

[*] Afterwards married to John Hooker.

lots and streets; but not more than one third of the streets are
yet opened; and of those which are opened, several have not
more than two or three buildings upon them. The State
House is placed on an eminence directly in the center of the
township, though very far from the center of the buildings.
The principal street is Richardson Street which runs on the
east side of the State House: although State Street which
runs on the west side was designed, by the commissioners who
planned the town, for the principal one. State Street is the
central one: and the State House though made with two fronts
was however so constructed as to present its handsomest front
to the west. Yet public choice has
so far disregarded the original plan
that State Street is, even to this
time, to a considerable extent, over-
run with bushes. That part of the
town which is not put into open
streets is, for the most part, a wilder-
ness of pines. Now and then is seen
a cultivated spot of a few acres
which forms an exception. The
State House is very large on the
ground, but yet so low as to be entirely void of anything like just proportion. It has only two stories;
and one of these is partly below the
natural surface of the ground, and is
of brick plaistered over. The lower
story is appropriated to the Treasurer's, Secretary's, and Surveyor
General's offices. There are several
other rooms, which, as far as I can learn, are used for little
else than lodging rooms for the goats that run loose about the
streets, and which, as the doors are never shut, have at all
times free access. The court house is a much handsomer
building—of brick, two stories high. There is only one church
in the town. The people think it "*a very neat, pretty building*";
but I am certain there is not a country parish in Connecticut,
but would disdain not to build a better one, in case they were
about to build at all. It is not more than one third as large as
Farmington Church; has no steeple; and the inside is in a very
coarse and unfinished state. It is not plaistered—and the
seats are merely movable benches placed promiscuously on the

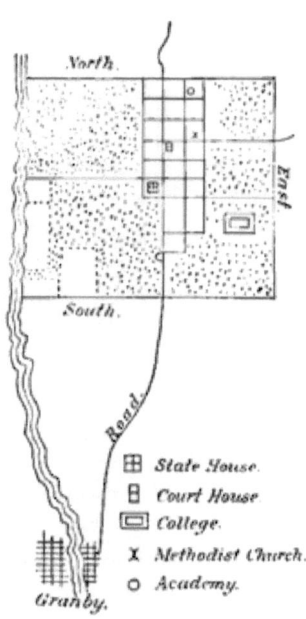

North.

East

South.

Road

Granby.

⊞ *State House.*
目 *Court House.*
▭ *College.*
X *Methodist Church.*
○ *Academy.*

floor. The pulpit and altar are finished and present a neat enough appearance. The same is true of the outside.—The houses generally are built of wood and many of them, though small, are pretty. These peculiarities distinguish them from Connecticut houses: They are generally narrower—having for the convenience of ventilation, only one tier of rooms. They are without cellars; being set up on blocks or stones considerably above the ground, and left open below the floors:—it being an opinion somewhat prevalent that cellars are unhealthy. They are unconnected with the kitchens. The chimneys are built and carried up, all the way, on the outside of the house.—The execution of all the work that I have noticed seems to me very different from that of Connecticut. Everything has a shackling, flimsy look—Joints are parting—Boards are coming off— Plaistering is full of cracks and breaks.

The number of houses and stores in the town I should judge to be over an hundred.—The inhabitants have no special privileges at present except a power of making regulations concerning the streets public wells and market, through the agency of a committee who are stiled "Commissioners of the Streets."[1] They are however expecting ere long to get from the legislature a charter of incorporation, which shall confer upon them the same powers with Camden and other little cities or boroughs.

Richardson Street and some others are lined, in part, with a beautiful tree called the Pride of India. In some few places a native pine is left standing, though they are every day diminishing in number. The inhabitants do not like them at all; and will not for a moment admit the idea that so cheap a tree as the pine which overruns their whole state can possibly contribute to the embellishment of a town. Hence they have commenced against them a "war of extermination". Around the State House are left standing some lofty forest oaks which afford a grateful shade, and give the scenery a rural and a charming cast.

The citizens as far as I can learn have a great variety of character. This is naturally to be expected when it is remembered that they are of such various origin. A few only are native Carolinians: some are from Virginia; some from New England—Some from England, Scotland and Ireland; some from France; some from various countries of the German Empire.

[1] This was by an act of 1798. Columbia was incorporated by act of December 19, 1805.

The fashions of dress, differ in some trifling particulars only from the fashions now prevailing in Connecticut. Suwarrow boots are much less worn, both here and in Charleston. Ruffles are more in use both at the bosom and the hands. The dress throughout is in general not so loose as in Conn.—As to the ladies' fashions, I don't know what they were when I left Conn., and I have never observed what they are here, any further than to notice with satisfaction, that their dresses are not so immodestly cut and put on, as those of the Northern fashionables.

The vehicles used here are peculiar in their construction. They are called chairs—designed for one horse—most of them without any spring except what is in the elasticity of the Shafts (as the thills are here universally called). Some have what are called cradle springs, placed, one under each shaft. They are all made without tops, and finished in a very plain manner. They cost I believe about one hundred dollars. The harnesses are made in a corresponding style. I don't believe there is a top chaise, or a silver plated harness in the whole town.

There is very little verdure in the town; the soil being too dry and sandy to produce grass. Consequently the streets are very deficient in that life and freshness of appearance which usually prevails in the towns of New England.

The public burying ground is in a pleasant and retired spot, east of the town—surrounded on three sides by copses of native pines which serve to render it suitably solemn. It has however a neglected appearance, not being enclosed by a fence, except in particular spots that have palings around the graves of particular families. These palings are almost the only monuments. A very few graves have wooden ones carved and painted in resemblance of stone, with inscriptions; and one or two have stones. I suppose the scarcity either of free-stone or marble is the reason of their using wood; for no part of the State that I have yet seen gives the smallest indication of the existence of such substances. Indeed regular stones of any quality are extremely scarce here; so that even the foundations of houses and the walls of wells, that have any walls at all, are made of brick. * * *

Returned and went with Mr. Chapman into the State House. The Senate and Representative chamber though not magnificent, are finished in a better style than the exterior of the edifice would authorize one to expect. They are furnished with handsome carpets, tables and chairs—with elegant maps of the U. S. and of each State in the Union—also of Europe and Asia—with a plan of Charleston and another of Columbia. The latter is executed with a pen in a very neat manner by a young Mr. Waring of this town who presented one to each house. The legislature in return made him a compliment of an hundred dollars.

There is considerable elegance, bordering on magnificence about the seats of the President of the Senate and Speaker of the House. The curtains for the windows, before which the chairs are placed on an elevated and commanding stand, are quite rich and beautiful to the eye. Those belonging to the seat of the former are of beautiful damask; were sent for to England and cost five hundred dollars.—In the Senate Chamber is a Legislative Library for the use of the members of both houses. It appears to have on the shelves, at present, about one hundred and fifty volumes. They consist to a considerable extent of Journals of the English Parliament, Journals of the U. S. Congress, and of some of the State legislatures and conventions, Acts of Congress, Statutes of the Several States, and political treatises. There is some history and some entertaining miscellany. Mr. C. tells me there is a considerable number of the books lost. Some being scattered about in town where the members have left them, and some being carried out of town. He says the legislature is very careless of the Library, doing very little more than to vote a supply of money occasionally to purchase books, which when purchased are often taken out without being charged, and retained for months and years without being demanded.

Observing, among the papers that lay scattered about the floor, several letters, I had the curiosity to pick up one. It proved to be a solicitation from a person in the low country to one of the members to lend him his vote and influence in procuring the Sheriffalty of one of the districts. It appeared to me so much of a curiosity as to be worth transcribing. Except the date, signature and address it was in print, and in the following form:

James Richbourgh Esqr.

Colleton District Nov. 15th. 1804

Dr Sir

intending to offer myself a candidate for the office of Sheriff for Colleton District at the next session of the Legislature, I take the liberty of soliciting the favor of your vote and influence to promote my election to the said office.

I refer you and your friends to Captain Hamilton,[1] the Comptroller-general, for any information you may think proper to be acquainted with respecting me; also to Colonel Pinckney, member of the Legislature from this District.

I am, sir, respectfully

Your most obedient servant

WM OSWALD.

James Richbourgh Esqr.

Expressing my surprise that such a mode of obtaining promotion should be resorted to, I was informed that offices are rarely bestowed by the Legislature without solicitation; for the State being so large, and the people so scattered, it cannot otherwise be known, who are candidates—and without this knowledge it would be a chance if offices should be given to those who would accept of them.

Tuesday Nov. 12th. * * * Had some conversation with Mr. Chapman on the comparative merit of the poor laws in Connecticut and this State. He says that many of the regulations and usages existing on this subject in New England are despised by the Carolinians, who have a high sense of liberty. They think such regulations an abridgment of natural liberty, and wonder how a man can "get along" to live there with so many restrictions. The practice of warning a poor, idle man out of town to prevent expense is considered an unrighteous meddling with another's concerns. In S. Carolina, as the poor are supported by the State altogether, no one town or county feels interested in sending them off, and an idle, worthless fellow is suffered to loiter about without having any questions asked, till, when a good opportunity presents, he perhaps steals a horse and rides off. The New England practice of placing an overseer over a man who squanders and dissipates his property, is condemned by the people here, who seem to think that as every man has a right to do what he pleases with his own, so the public have no right to interfere in his affairs.

Friday Nov. 15. Took a ride with brother in the forenoon down to the Granby ferry, and thence along by the side of the Congaree, two or three miles further. On an elevated second bank of the river, eight or ten rods from the water, on a pleasant spot, amid a grove of tall Lombardy poplars stands the house of Charles Pinckney, Esq. our minister at the Court of

---

[1] Paul Hamilton (1762–1816), comptroller 1799–1804, governor 1804–1806, Secretary of the Navy 1809–1813.

Madrid. It is two large stories high, square, with a small portico in front, not very elegant, and in appearance rather ancient and neglected. An office of brick, with a cupola stands a few yards from the left end, among the trees. The appearance is solemn and gloomy—the mansion being shut up, and not a person to be seen, any where near. His plantation which lies on the river, above and below the house, is very valuable, but the estate has not been perfectly well managed during Mr. P's absence, and it is now, as it was indeed before his departure, very much embarrassed with debt. A heavy judgment was recovered against him not long since, and on the day of my arrival in Columbia, a number of his slaves were sold by the Sheriff to satisfy the execution.—Passing through Mr. P's, we rode about half a mile into Col. Hampton's plantation, which adjoins it below. Returned another way, and visited a cotton gin, about which a number of negroes were at work, very busily in cleaning the cotton from its seeds. I had no conception till now of the immense benefit produced to the Southern States by the invention of the ingenious Mr. Whitney of New Haven. The seeds adhere to the staple (as the woolly part or thread of the cotton is called) with a great deal of tenacity, and used formerly to be picked out by hand. Now, the gins of Mr. W. are in universal use. They are put in operation by a horse or by water. A first rate one, put in motion by two horses, and well attended by a man and two boys, will, it is said, clean as much in a day, as two thousand negroes can do, in the old way. If one quarter of this is true, the saving of labor must be prodigious.

Saturday Nov. 16th. * * * Enquiring the reason why European goods are sold so much higher in this state than at the Northward, I was informed that the merchants of Carolina are less punctual, and more frequently bankrupts—that the planters have money only once a year, viz. after selling their crops,—and of course the merchants trust a great deal; * * *

Sun. Nov. 17th. Brother J. with a number of other lawyers set out this morning for Winnsborough to attend the court which sits there to-morrow. They all started together in chairs; and, with their servants on horseback, behind, formed quite a

¹ Charles Pinckney (1758-1824) member of the Convention of 1787, governor of South Carolina 1789-1792, 1796-1798, 1806-1808. Senator 1797-1801, was envoy to Spain from 1802 to October, 1805.

procession.—It did not seem easy to reconcile all this noise and
bustle of Sunday journeying, with my New-Eng⁴ principles.
However, the Carolinians do not seem to be very scrupulous
on this subject; and unfortunately they find too easy an excuse
for the thing in the very laws of the land. These laws do not
expressly authorize violations of the Sabbath; but they fairly
invite such violations in various ways: Particularly in the
appointment of public occasions, which are usually on Mon
days. Thus the legislature begins its session on Monday. The
college Commencement is assigned to Monday; and all the
courts in the State are opened on Monday. In the assignment
of court-time there is this further peculiarity: For the courts
in the country, only one week each is allowed. Hence it frequently happens that the same judge and the same lawyers
who are detained at one Court till Saturday night, are obliged,
by this arrangement, to attend another court, 20, 30 or 40 miles
distant, the next Monday Morning: and how to accomplish
this, without encroaching on the Sabbath, might puzzle even
an ingenious lawyer.   *   *   *

Mon. Nov. 18. The sessions of the legislature and the Court
of Common pleas both commence this day. The town of
course assumes a busy appearance. Great numbers of people
are flocking in; both men and women. There do not appear
to be any circumstances of unusual parade attending the meeting of the legislature: but the members get together at the
State House very leisurely, lounge about a while, and at length
count their numbers. If a quorum is on the ground, the
houses form themselves and send notice to each other and to
the governor. If there is'nt a quorum, so much the better, as
I should judge by the conduct of a number of the members,
who appear to take more satisfaction in figuring about in the
streets, and in the piazzas of their boarding houses, and in
being looked upon as public men, than in the thought of being
confined to the toil of public business. I am told it is not an
uncommon thing for three or four days to elapse before the
business of the session is begun.

I was not a little surprised by the novelty exhibited in the
sitting of the court, and the concomitant circumstances. I
had never felt any interest in the sessions of the courts at
New Haven, nor looked forward to the time as to an event of
any importance: indeed, I seldom used to know when a court
of any grade was to be opened, until I heard the court-house

bell announcing that public business of some kind or other
was to be attended to. With such feelings of indifference I
had many times wondered at the interest excited among the
people here, by the approach of court-time. "*Well sir, the
court draws near*", one neighbor would observe to another a
fortnight or three weeks beforehand. The reasons seem to be
that courts are held but seldom, and continued but a short
time; that more people are of course concerned in the proceedings—that more jury-men are called, and more court officers required to attend. The company that crowds into town
also makes business for the boarding houses and taverns, and
thus cause a *pecuniary* interest to be felt by a considerable
number of the inhabitants.

This court is, I believe, known in law by the name of Court
of Common Pleas. This title however, does not sufficiently
designate its character, which would be better understood by
calling it the Court of Common law, in opposition to Court of
Equity; for it has as much the powers of the English Court of
Kings Bench as of the Common pleas. Its jurisdiction is very
extensive, including all criminal cases whatever, both small
and great, and all civil cases which are beyond the jurisdiction of a justice of the peace; that is, cases of debt or assump-
sit, in which the sum demanded does not exceed twelve dollars. It has also a power of deciding summarily, and without
the intervention of a jury (unless one of the parties wish it)
in cases where the demand is less than 75 dollars. In these
summary processes as they are called, there is much less regard
paid to legal formalities:—the parties may be examined on
oath, and the judge has more latitude in deciding on equitable
principles. A single judge holds this court. From his deci-
sion an appeal lies, on points of law, to the whole bench collected, consisting of six judges.

The courts here are attended with more ceremony than in
Connecticut. The judge is dressed in a large, black, silk
gown, and wears a band: and he is attended by the sheriff to
and from the court. The lawyers also, while at the bar, are
required by the rules of court to wear black coats and black
gowns. The sheriff's deputy and six or eight constables are
required to attend court. The latter are stationed in different
parts of the house, with their long staves, to enforce good order
and wait the commands of the judge. The business of the
court is often preceded by a sermon; to defray the expence of

which, money is appropriated by law. I believe about 10 or 12 dollars are allowed for each sermon. For some reason or other, it was, at this time omitted.—Most of the forenoon was taken up in forming juries and calling cases. I was not a little amused with the oddness of many names that were called; particularly those of the German inhabitants; of whom there is a considerable number in this district. Some, whose names in the original German were rather awkward and harsh to an English ear, have, instead of softening them, and by some slight and unessential change adapting them to the English idiom, resorted to the singular expedient of translating them, and exchanging them for such English words as they most nearly signify. Such are the names of Turnip-seed and Schoon-maker.

The present occasion enabled me to learn something of the appearance, character, and manners of the great mass of the country people in these parts. The contrast between them and the Columbians is very striking. They are indeed a rude, unpolished race. They are, both men and women, almost without exception, dressed in coarse homespun cotton of a mixed color. There is nothing like fashion, taste or refinement about them. The women wore short loose-gowns and petticoats, and sun-bonnets of the same cloth. They were standing about in public places all day, gaping and staring at every body and every thing that was in any degree new to them. Some of the women had crying children in their arms. There were many girls of 18 or 20, who, with other women showed so little diffidence or sense of decency as to crowd up to the bar among the multitude, and even step up on the benches behind the lawyers to look over their shoulders. The street was full of hucksters' waggons and stalls as on public days in Connecticut.

Tues. Nov. 19. * * * The presiding judge is Thomas Waties, Esq. of Sumpter District.[1] He appears to be about fifty years old:—has much apparent meekness in his countenance, and exhibits, throughout, a dignified demeanor. Sitting himself, he gives his charges to the jury sitting. This, he does in plain, familiar terms; in a manner quite modest, and free from ostentation. Judge W. is thought to have a greater store of legal knowledge than any other judge on the bench:—but

[1] Thomas Waties (1760–1828) was an associate judge of the Court of Appeals from 1785 to 1811, of the Court of Equity from 1811 to 1824, and of the law courts again from 1824 to 1828. O'Neall, Bench and Bar of South Carolina, I. 43, 44.

some of the lawyers are unwilling to allow him full credit for candor.

Wedn. Nov. 20. Mr. Egan spoke nearly two hours in court:—appeared much engaged:—did not leave the case perfectly clear, but rather clouded by the multiplicity of his views and reasonings.—I suppose he felt as if his side was a precarious one. Mr. Nott[1] spoke about 20 minutes in reply. His method was clear; his language perspicuous and without the least embellishment:—his manner moderate, modest and unaffected.—Mr. N. is a native of Conn. and a graduate of Y. Coll. He once represented one of the upper districts of this state in Congress; but gave his constituents offence by voting for Burr in preference to Jefferson, and was from that time left out of civil office. The judge, in his charge to the jury alluded to Egan's long and intricate speech, intimating that there had been an unnecessary waste of time, and cautioned them against being led from the plain course of rectitude by what had been importunately and artfully urged by one of the counsel. The legislature have not yet made a quorum.   *   *   *

Friday Nov. 22nd. The court finished its business last evening and adjourned. The time has been short yet much business has been accomplished. It is a common saying that the Carolinians are industrious in nothing but law business. Whatever might be the case as to the truth of the general remark, I was now convinced that the exception was properly made. The judge rarely adjourns the court for dinner, and he tolerates no delay on any account whatever. If a jury-man, or an officer of the court is not at his post in due season, he is reprimanded or fined. Two setts of jurymen are kept in readiness, so that as soon as one has retired to make a verdict, the other may begin to try a new cause.   *   *   *

Saturday Nov. 23.   *   *   * The senate made a quorum this morning. The other house, in order to do it, found it necessary to send out their messenger to request the attendance of such members as he might find scattered about the town. Among other places, he came to the office to find Mr. Egan. Egan was very busy just then in arranging some court papers, and not a little perplexed with the multiplicity of his avocations. "*Mr. Egan*" said the messenger "*the members present their compliments, and request the favor of your attendance at*

[1] Abraham Nott, Yale 1788, Member of Congress 1799–1801, afterwards (1810–1830) a law judge. O'Neall, II. 121, 122.

the House". "*I am very busily employed*" said Egan: "*I don't see how I can go*". The messenger replied; "*They want only one or two more to make a quorum, and they're very anxious to organise the House*". "*I can't help it*", was the reply, "*you must go to somebody else*". "*I fear they can't get a quorum without you*". "*Well, D—n the quorum—I tell you it's impossible for me to go over.*" Thus ended the Dialogue. However, they succeeded in collecting a sufficient number without him, and proceeded to business. Mr. W. C. Pinckney the standing speaker being absent, a new one was elected viz. Mr. Joseph Alston a beauish young man of about 28, from Georgetown.[1] A committee of three was sent out to inform him. They returned in a few minutes and in a ceremonious style conducted him to the desk and introduced him into the Speaker's chair. He entered the room draped in a long black silk gown, the Speaker's habit;[2] and after having taken the chair, rose and made a short speech of two minutes. He appeared at first considerably embarrassed; yet spoke pertinently. A considerable number of the members appear very young. Very few appear to be more than 50 years old. They differ very much in age, dialect, dress and manners. Some have showy and costly dress; but not a small number are plain. rustic sort of folk dressed in their own manufactures. Some speak like foreigners, as they probably are: Some have the polished language of the Charlestonians: and some the coarse and more blunt language of the mountaineers. The lower house (as is customary I understand) appointed a chaplain to perform divine service on Sundays, and by a large majority voted him 100 dlls for his services. A few were opposed to the motion. One plain-looking old fellow with flapt hat and each hand in a pocket, got up hastily, and in rather an ill humored tone said "*Let them that go to hear him put their hands in their pockets and pay him themselves.*" The house adjourned at noon, because it was found, in the midst of their business, that some members having gone off, a sufficient number was not left for a quorum. Thus ends a week of Carolina legislation! * * *

Tues, Nov. 26. Very busy all the morning in writing briefs and affidavits, in preparation for the Court of Appeals which begins its Session to-day. These briefs are concise statements

[1] Speaker throughout the time of Hooker's residence in Columbia.

[2] By a resolution passed this session December 19, 1805, provision was made for the Speaker's wearing hereafter a gown of blue satin trimmed with white ermine.

of the cases carried up from a single judge's court to the full bench, and are in some respects a substitute for writs of error. Writs of error are not known in this state. These briefs are usually of such length as to fill half a sheet; and there must be as many copies of each one as there are judges on the bench.—After this went over to the State House. I am fond of resorting thither occasionally because it is a relaxation from the fatigue of writing, and because it affords me one of the best opportunities for learning the Carolinian character. It is not difficult to see that the Carolinians are fond of acting in public affairs—of figuring in debate—of having, or appearing to have an influence in measures of State. There are a great many of the members who can't sit easy, without having an agency in all that is doing. It is disgusting to see such ignorant men as some of them are continually putting in a word, making motions, or objecting to them; and all without any apparent reason except to make a noise and get notice. But it all passes well enough. Good patriotism! Sublime efforts in their country's cause! Perhaps they think with Sallust; "*Pulchrum est bene facere reipublicae; etiam bene dicere haud absurdum est*". Mr. John Taylor,[1] who represents the Election district of Saxe Gotha on the other side of the Congaree, but who lives in this town, was among the most sensible of those who spoke today. He argued about 10 or 12 minutes very earnestly against the propriety of allowing the Gov. to communicate his information to a committee of the House, instead of laying it before the House at large. He thought such an allowance would be an undue approximation towards an union of the Executive and legislative powers. His language was good; but he deviated in some measure from the point in question. Mr. Wm. Lowndes of Charleston,[2] a young man of perhaps 26, in a short, but very luminous speech replied; and was attended to by a remarkably silent house.

The members sit with their hats on; only taking them off when they rise to speak. Their number I imagine is not more than half as great as that of the lower house in Conn.[3] Questions are decided not by holding up hands but by acclamation. * * *

---

[1] Major John Taylor (1770-1832), member of Congress 1807-1810, of the United States Senate 1810-1816, of Congress 1816-1817, governor of South Carolina 1826-1828.

[2] William Lowndes (1782-1822) afterwards famous as a prominent member of Congress 1811-1822, and noted from early youth for sagacity in public affairs.

[3] Their number was 124.

Wedn. Nov. 27. Attended the Court of Appeals this forenoon. This Court is sometimes called the constitutional court;
I suppose from the circumstances of its taking the constitu-
tion for its primary guide, and setting aside such decisions as
are founded on unconstitutional Statutes for this is a right
insisted on by this court, and one which has been within a
short time, executed.[1] The judges are all dressed in black
robes, wear bands, and make a venerable appearance. They
sit with their hats on or off, as inclination or accident requires.
Their names are Grimke and Bay of Charleston, Waties of
Statesburg, Brevard of Camden, Tresevant of Charleston, and
Wilds of Darlington district.[2] Mr. Wilds is very young: not
over thirty two, it is said—and the most popular judge in
the State.

Thurs. Nov. 28. Went into the Senate Chamber. The Senate appears rather more venerable than the other house; but
there is not that Striking difference, which I had expected to
see; and which I had been accustomed to see between the two
branches of the Conn. Legislature. A few of them appear
very young, for so high a station—They are 36 in number, and
sit in three concentric semicircles fronting the President.[3]
The Pres. wears a long light blue satin robe, edged with white
fur. The members are for the most part quite ordinary men
in point of talents, though they are men of property. A few
are lawyers and physicians; but most of them are planters.
The leading Senators are Mr. Ward (the Pres.) of Charleston,
Col. Barnwell of Beaufort, Mr. Smith of Yorkville, Mr. Stark
of this town, and Mr. Izard of Goose-Creek.[4] In the lower
house, Mr. Keating Simons, a lawyer of Charleston, Mr. W.
Smith[5] a lawyer also from the same place, Mr. Cochran the
Intendant of the city, Mr. Henry Deas a merchant, Mr. David
Deas, once a lawyer (both living in Charleston, but I believe
representing some country place) Maj. John Taylor of Colum-
bia. Mr. Eagen of Columbia, Mr. Evans, of Winnsborough and
Speaker Alston are among the ablest men, but do not all take

[1] In White v. Kendrick, 1 Brevard 469, at the session next preceding this, April, 1805.

[2] John Faucheraud Grimké, Elihu Hall Bay, Thomas Waties, Joseph Brevard, Lewis C.
Trezevant, Samuel Wilds.   See O'Neall, Vol. 1.

[3] At this time, John Ward.

[4] John Ward; Robert Barnwell (1762-1814); William Smith (1762-1840) judge 1808-1816,
U. S. Senator 1817 1823, 1826-1830, the opponent of Calhoun; Robert Stark (1762-1830)
state solicitor; further characterizations of most of these will be found later; lives of
most of them are given in O'Neall's Bench and Bar of South Carolina.

[5] William Loughton Smith (1758-1812) member of Congress 1789-1797, minister to Portugal and Spain.

an active part. The most active of these are Simons, Smith the two Taylors, the two Deas and Alston. There is another sett who are up very often, and although of inferior, and some of them even of contemptible talents, yet they are not without influence. Such are Col. Hill, a very old man from York, D. E. Huger (pronounced Hugee) from Georgetown, Mr. Johnson from Edgefield, Col. Mays from Cambridge, Maj. Miles from the neighborhood of Savannah, A. B. Stark from Granby, John Izard Wright from near Beaufort. Several of these are however, men of good sense, though not well educated, nor extensively informed.

Friday Nov. 29. * * * It is not an uncommon thing in this state for foreigners to be promoted to civil offices. Several are in the State legislature; and they have in several instances been sent to Congress. Mr. O'Brien Smith,[1] who is elected a member of Congress in Col. Hampton's stead is an Irish gentleman of great property in the low country. He is said to be very friendly and useful to any of his countrymen that apply to him, however mean their condition may be; and provided they conduct uprightly, and prove friendly to our government, he takes a pleasure in patronising them. He is tall, strait, portly and robust—genteel in appearance, and resembling considerably Col. David Humphreys of Conn.[2]

Sat. Nov. 30. * * * The Federal court sat today; but there being no causes before it, the two juries were immediately dismissed, without receiving any charge, and the court adjourned. Judge Bee attended.[3] * * *

Mon. Dec. 2nd. The important question of the slave-trade came on today in the House of Representatives, in a Committee of the whole. The principal speakers on the subject were Simons, Speaker Alston, Miles, Taylor (of Pendleton) and Wright.[4] Some others made occasional observations. Simons and Alston were for shutting the ports, the other three against it. The advocates for the prohibition did honor to themselves and their cause by their eloquence and the liberality and cor-

---

[1] Member of Congress, 1805-1807.

[2] Col. David Humphreys (1752-1818) aid-de-camp of Washington, minister to Portugal 1791-1796, to Spain 1796-1802.

[3] Thomas Bee, judge of the United States District Court for the district of South Carolina.

[4] By successive enactments, from 1787 to 1803, the importation of slaves into South Carolina had been prohibited. These laws were repealed December 17, 1803, and importation remained legal until January 1, 1808, when it became illegal by Act of Congress. Du Bois, Suppression of the Slave Trade. 229-240, 245. In four years 39,075 slaves were brought in at Charleston. Charleston Year Book, 1880, p. 263.

rectness of their principles. Maj. Taylor on the other side did
as well as the nature of the cause would permit. Simons' language was choice and elegant, his expression clear and perspicuous, his gestures graceful and animated. But there is too
much appearance of study in his whole manner. He dwelt a
little on the true policy of the System, as it respects the money
making part of it—much on the danger to be feared from the
number of blacks in the country—much on the injustice and
inhumanity of the traffic. He continued perhaps 20 minutes.
There was a variety in his delivery that engaged attention:
for he sometimes spoke very loud, and sometimes, particularly in ending his sentences, hardly raised his voice above a
whisper. He had, in the course of his speech, several sudden
exclamations which would have been more moving, had they
been a little more natural. It was a very regular, well constructed, and elegant speech. I presume it was previously prepared, if not written at full length, for the occasion. Alston's
speech appeared to me more like an extemporaneous one, though
it is said by such as are acquainted with him, that he always,
without exception, writes his speeches. He, like Simons, used
notes; but did not recur to them so often; nor did he confine
himself so much to method, nor avoid so scrupulously every
expression not stamp'd with elegance: yet his arrangement
was not bad, nor his language undignified. He did not, at
first, speak with uncommon fluency: indeed he stammered a
little; but when he became once fairly engaged, his words
appeared to flow with the greatest ease. His figures and
allusions, were eminently striking and beautiful, and his
speech abounded with them. He dropped some excellent
moral and political sentiments, quoted two or three texts of
sublime morality from the scriptures, and with great vehemency
and apparent sincerity urged the house to consult the dictates
of justice, and humanity, in opposition to sordid interest. His
manner of delivery was extremely good,—and his gestures
forcible and expressive. He labored sometime, and with success, to shew that the increase of slaves tends to destroy that
equality which is the basis of our republican institutions, and
insisted that it is not only unjust to bring them in, but demon-
strably injurious to the real interests of the State. In his
argument was a fund of good sense and useful information.
The utmost silence pervaded the house while he spoke thirty
five or forty minutes. Mr. Alston is a short man, and rather

thick. Of a dark complexion—with thick, black hair and a formidable pair of whiskers that cover a great part of his face, and nearly meet, at the chin. His dress and demeanor are well deserving the name of *buckish*. When not in the legisla tive hall, he may be seen, as often as any where, about the stables, looking at fine horses, dressed in a short jockey like surtout or frock, and laced and tossled boots, with a segar in his mouth, and with much more of the "gig and tandem" levity, than of the austere virtues of a senatorial leader. In deed he is one of the last persons that I should have picked out from the crowd of people in town, for a president of one branch of the legislature.

Major Miles is a fat looking, but well built man of perhaps forty five, from Prince William parish, and cavalry officer in the militia, as I judge from his frequent motions, resolutions, talks &c. relative to that subject. He shows much of a vain, forward demeanor, and is pretty independent: but I have as yet seen no display of abilities by him, to justify his forwardness. In the present case he was evidently under disadvantages, by being enlisted on a bad side of the question. The resolution under consideration as drawn up by Mr. Alston was prefaced with several considerations, which Miles and some others could not get over: such as the inconsistency of the slave trade with the precepts of Christianity—with justice, humanity &c., and lastly with the true interest of the State. Miles was for con sidering the question only in the light last mentioned, and could not see the propriety of prefacing the resolve with con siderations of religion, justice, and humanity: "for" says he "Nobody on this floor doubts that; and therefore we ought only to ask "*Is it for our interest to shut the ports?* We did not come here to debate on what makes for or against religion, but what makes for or against the interest of our constitu |ents|". He then attempted to shew that the smuggling of negroes would be the consequence of shutting the ports,—and that the upper country would not have equal privileges with the lower, if now, when they are fast becoming rich enough to buy slaves, they are prevented by the laws, while the lower country are already supplied. Maj. Taylor took a different and much less odious way: and exhibited in his argument considerable candor. He said he had once advocated the shutting of the ports, but he thought it impracticable now to prevent smuggling, without building some *revenue vessels:* and

as the general government would doubtless take up the sub
ject after two years more he thought it best for the State to let
the matter rest, and meanwhile give the upper country planters an opportunity, by purchasing more slaves, to be on a more
equal footing with their fellow citizens in the lower country.
He reasoned coolly and dispassionately, and addressed the
understanding in plain, perspicuous, and handsome language;
though there was too much monotony in his delivery. A
majority of the house, I was gratified to find, were so much
swayed by a sense of justice, as to pass the resolution.

Tues. Dec. 3rd. Attended the debates of the Senate part of
the day, and had the pleasure of hearing Mr. John Ward, a
lawyer of Charleston. A more pleasing speaker, I have rarely
heard. When he is engaged in something which he has previously considered, and that he fully understands, there is
nothing to diminish the pleasure of the hearer, unless it be the
extreme slowness of his utterance. There is however nothing
of that pain which is felt in attending to a speaker who is at a
loss for words: for one soon learns that he has at command a
rich stock of words, and ideas: and that the hesitancy which
he discovers, is the result of deliberate good sense formed into
a habit: for it does not take place in such parts of a sentence
as are strictly connected, but only between the members of the
sentences and between the sentences themselves. He speaks
entirely in the Sheridanian dialect, which is, as far as I have
observed, much the most common dialect of well educated
Charlestonians.—Mr. W. is a small man—pleasant and facetious disposition—penetrating look—quick and graceful motion—dignified when in the chair of the Senate, but a little prone
to levity when out of it. So able an orator as he is, it seems
unfortunate that he should in any degree injure that influence
which he might possess, by sometimes taking his side too
hastily on an unimportant question, and speaking, though very
beautifully, yet with too little judgment. Mr. W. was, till
lately, President of the Senate, but being obliged to be absent
a part of the time, resigned the chair, and was succeeded by
Col. Robert Barnwell. Col. B. is a tall, portly, well built man
of about sixty years—a man of singular gravity, and possessed
of great influence in the Senate. Said to be an eminent orator,
and a very religious character. An attempt was once made,
though without any success, to debar him from holding a seat
in the legislature on the ground of his being a preacher, because

he had one summer, while his minister was gone on a journey
for his health, read the service in the church, and sometimes
exhorted the audience. He resembles considerably Gen.
Wyllys of Hartford.[1] Mr. Stark has a thundering, overbearing, positive manner of speaking resembling (except the squeak-
ing part) in tone and delivery Henry R. Storrs.[2] * * *

Wedn. Dec. 4th. * * * The commencement exhibition of
the newly instituted college in this place was held this evening.
I attended it, and found considerable entertainment. The only
junior the Sophomores and Freshmen, exhibited pieces, some
selected and some composed by themselves. They consisted
of one Latin and one Greek oration, Declamations, and Dialogues. Most of the subjects were trite and common, such as
the benefits of education, the necessity of knowledge in a republic, the vanity of riches, pleasures, &c. as the means of happiness—but the performances were all decent, considering
circumstances, and some of them very handsome in style,
sentiment and delivery. Some of the Dialogues were replete
with humor. Each of the performances was applauded by
clapping hands and drumming with the feet.

Thurs. Dec. 5th. After spending an hour or two at the office
this forenoon, went over to the Representative's chamber and
heard Messrs David Deas (pronounced Days) Wm. Lowndes
and Gist[3] speak on the subject of Capt. Rowse's petition.[4] Deas
had a loud, vehement, overbearing manner of delivery, though
his voice is not heavy, uses fewer gestures than most of the
Speakers and takes very little pains to polish his language.
He is however a pretty good speaker. I understand he is a
lawyer of some note in Charleston, and represents one of the
country parishes.

Lowndes has a very soft, mild voice, speaks low but very distinctly and clearly—has a remarkably, candid, sincere, unsus-
picious manner of addressing himself to the house—a manner
so engaging as to command an universal silence. He does not
ornament his speech with flowers, and is altogether natural and
unaffected. He gestures but very little, having other means

---

[1] Samuel Wyllys (1739-1823), general of militia, at this time secretary of the State of
Connecticut.

[2] Henry R. Storrs (1787-1837), who had been in the class above Hooker at Yale, was a
member of Congress from New York, 1819-1831.

[3] Joseph Gist, member of the legislature 1803-1821, member of Congress, 1821-1827.
O'Neall, II. 219.

[4] See Acts of 1805, pp. 100-102. Rowse, being a senior captain in a militia regiment,
claimed the right to draw lots with another captain for the vacant position of major.

to engage attention, viz, plain and intelligible, yet very choice language, good sense, concise thoughts and expressions, clear method, and a lucid illustration of the point which he attempts. He is not at all forward in the house, but when he does rise, invariably to some purpose, and exhibits some views of the subject which had been overlooked by others. Gist (pronounced Ghist) is a lawyer of some repute from the back country, who, though without any thing like polish of diction, commonly speaks to the purpose, and has considerable merit as a speaker. Deas and Gist were in favor of annulling the Governor's proceeding in the case of Capt. Rowse. Lowndes was against any legislative interference in the case.   *   *   *

Frid, Dec. 6th. In the H. of R. today, Mr. Henry Deas of Charleston distinguished himself by an eloquent speech on Capt. Rowse's case. He was of opinion that it is a question determinable by a military tribunal, and one that the Legislature could not interfere with, on either ground, of right or policy. He was very animated, energetic, clear and concise. His gestures were very forcible, and not without expression, his language choice but not flowery—his voice loud and thundering. I think, I like his oratory better, considering all circumstances, than that of any one whom I have before heard. Mr. D. is said to be an uncommonly well informed legislator on questions of Banks, insurances, incorporations and subjects of that nature, but on questions in general does not often take an active part. Maj. Miles took a warm part in the debate in favor of Capt. Rowse. When the final vote was taken, a considerable majority appeared in favor of accepting the report of the Committee of the whole, which report was in favor of Rowse.

Sat. Dec. 7th. Assisted in making up judgments &c. at the office, till one o'clock:—then went into the senate and heard part of the debate on the subject of establishing free schools throughout the state.[1] The excellent Col. Barnwell, in a committee of the whole, spoke upon it with a great deal of good sense, good reasoning and eloquence. Indeed he is considered one of the greatest orators in the state. He has a heavy, sonorous voice which completely fills the room. It is somewhat rolling, and has in it something similar to Gov. Treadwell's of Connecticut, though more smooth and pleasant. His gestures are principally with extended arms, quite expressive

[1] The bill seems not to have passed.

and graceful, but not accompanied by so many flourishes as
Alston's. His manner of speaking is extremely natural and
engaging. With a dignified animation highly becoming such
a man and such a cause, he argued for the extension of the
means of education to every section of the country. You talk
much, says he, of the importance of having courts of justice
established in all parts of your land, that crimes may be *pun-
ished*: why not strike out the root of the evil by extending the
means of education, that your children may learn to read the
Bible, and be instructed in the great principles of morality,
and thus crimes be prevented? · Col. B. also proved himself a
good statesman by the remarks he made on the resources of
the State, and its ability now and in future to accomplish
objects of the kind proposed. Like Dr. Dwight, he seemed to
think that large bodies of men, such [as] a legislature for
example, are the worst of money managers.—With such views,
he moved to strike out of the bill a certain clause, in which the
Legislature were about to give some minute directions about
this State's share of the U. S. stock for the use of schools:—he
insisting that in case the management of it should be left to
the Comptroller General instead of the Legislature, the issue
of the business would undoubtedly be advantageous; but that
nothing could be more impolitic than for the legislature,
through excess of jealousy or distrust, to undertake the management of such complicated money matters themselves. His
motion was acceded to, though the bill itself, for some reason
or other did not exactly suit the members. One or two attempts
have formerly been made to accomplish this desirable object,
but they have not succeeded. I cannot learn however, that the
failures are owing to any hostility to the scheme: on the contrary, everybody seems to be in favor of it: but the difficulty
of concentrating the views of the members in any one satis-
factory plan has, more than any one thing else probably been
the cause. The evils of a sparse population are in this respect
now brought out to view, and the utility of such a system of
settlement in towns and villages as prevails in New England
is strikingly apparent.   *   *   *

December 9th. Wrote very steadily in the office till two o'clock
in the afternoon, when I felt quite fatigued enough to go into
the State House for recreation. The Senate were debating on
the Slave trade. Mr. Izard spoke with much ingenuity in favor
of *keeping open the ports.* Though possest of much mercantile,

and geographical knowledge, and some literature, he cannot be called a good speaker. His language is proper and flows with sufficient ease; but like many other members, who are probably either foreigners, or else accustomed to associate with foreigners, he is not easily understood by one [unused] to such foreign dialects. His gestures are easy enough, but rather singular; and are usually made with arms not widely extended, by sometimes clasping the hands, and at other times by bringing the back of the right hand with a slap into the palm of the left. There is another peculiarity in his action. Every half minute he retreats back two or three steps from his chair (which he commonly places before him while speaking) and then after standing so a short time, with two or three sprightly and graceful steps advances again to his place. Occasionally, he takes his steps sideways instead of back and forth—These motions are not entirely agreeable, because not adapted to any good purpose, yet they appear to be the result of vehement feelings in the speaker, and not of affectation. When I went in, he was speaking on the question of interest; and attempting to shew that the scarcity of specie in the country is not owing to the Slave trade, but to the exportation of dollars to Great Britain, where a high premium is given for them to carry on the East India trade with, and also to the East India trade itself as carried on by Americans,—particularly the New Englanders. He spoke with some humor on the enterprise of the New Englanders in "sallying out from every little village where a boat of a few tons burthen, and that will hold five Yankeys can come up, and entering on East India voyages with a little ginseng to barter with, and the rest of the cargo in dollars." In stating the inducements which exist for the exportation of specie thither, he observed that the population is so great in China, it cannot be increased—and public officers are appointed to go about the streets every morning, and bury or throw into the rivers the bodies of infants that have been cast out. This immense population makes the price of labor so very small that we in America and G. B. who are accustom'd to such high wages and prices, can't have any conception of it. I have seen, says he, a black silk vest that any beau in the State would be proud to wear, sold in Canton for seven pence (12½ cents) and a complete suit of nankeen from head to shoulders sold for half a dollar.

Dec. 10th. Visited the Senate chamber this morning, and heard a debate on the constitutionality and propriety of having the judges of Equity and the judges of the Common pleas ex-officiis Trustees of the State College.[1] Mr. Izard made a handsome speech in favor of it—it was very luminous, full of good sense, and very creditable to himself. He animadverted very pointedly on the republicanism of those members who were for excluding from the goverment of the College this learned body of men, and having their places filled by nobody knows who, according to the caprice of the legislature in their quatrennial appointments—Mr. Ward also spoke on the subject, and insisted that not only the judges, but also the President of the College, should by all means belong, as a matter of course to the corporation. It gave me pleasure to hear the case of the college in my State brought up as a precedent for the latter measure. It is the case I believe, says Mr. Ward, in all the New England colleges, that the President, ex-officio, holds a seat in the Board. In Yale College, he is not only a member, but occasionally presides in the Board. I well remember, when I was at New Haven, that Dr. Dwight was considered next in rank to the governor, and in Mr. Trumbull's absence, presided in the Board of that College.

This day had been appointed for a military parade in town. There had been so much previous talk about it, that I was induced to expect something grand. Two regiments, one of infantry, and one of cavalry, had been ordered out but only about half the infantry, and only one company (20 or 25 in number) of the cavalry made their appearance on the ground. I presume the whole number did not exceed 230 men. To one accustomed to view the martial spirit of the Connecticut militia, their appearance was wretched beyond belief. The Governor, with his three aids and private Secretary, accompanied also by Gen. M'Pherson, reviewed the regiment. They were all richly dressed, handsomely mounted, and riding by with heads uncovered, made an august appearance. Two of the aids were Marshall Cochran the Intendant of Charleston,[2] and Col. Warren who having lost a leg at the battle of Germantown, was attended by a servant on horseback bearing his crutches. Adjutant Gen. Earle who is paid

[1] By act of December 14, 1805 (Acts of 1805, pp. 82-84) the judges of the common pleas were added to the board of trustees of the college.

[2] Charles B. Cochran was intendant of Charleston this year. Charleston Year Book, 1881, p. 369.

by the State for attending all the reviews, was on the ground
from the beginning, to see the regiment formed. He then
instructed the officers how to perform some evolutions, and
assigned them their several posts. Exercised the regiment in
marching, wheeling &c. and had the chief command. He is
an excellent officer, and exhibits a handsome appearance.
Bears the rank and title of Colonel. Col. Meyer (pronounced
Myers) the Commandant of the Reg't. rode an indifferent
horse appeared very awkward and evidently understood little
or nothing about his business. He is such a simpleton that
when once administering the oath in a sort of Court Martial,
he read the whole form as it stands in the Statute Book
including the Quaker proviso—thus " *You A. B. do solemnly
swear (or affirm as the case may be) that the evidence you now
give in, is true &c.* Maj. Clifton appeared advantageously,
though a clubfooted Major could not fail to strike an observer
as an incongruity.—Maj. Sheppard rides an ordinary, steady
old white horse, with a plain saddle, one girt and single bridle.
No holsters, no saddle cloth, and no unusual apparatus about
his steed. He is a pleasant featured young man of about 28
or 30—very modest and still on parade, makes no exertions,
and probably knows little about military discipline. The Cap-
tains, four in number, were in regimentals, and with some of
the subalterns appeared decently: but two or three of the
Lieutenants or Ensigns had neither uniforms, nor arms.
Another of the subalterns, had a gun, cartouch box and bay-
onet, but no part of the military dress. The Artillery men,
about sixteen in number, with one brass field piece, were in
uniform. Besides these there was not a foot soldier (save one
or two, and they were probably serjeants or Corporals), in
regimentals. The non-commissioned officers generally, were
not only without military dress and insignia, but ordinarily,
and some of them even meanly dressed. Several of them were
without guns, and more without cartouch boxes. But the soldiers! O foul disgrace to a free republic! the soldiers seemed,
literally, a herd of ragamuffins—Dressed for the most part,
very meanly and as many as one in every eight or ten, without
either gun, flint, cartouch box or any thing characteristic of a
soldier—At least half of them with gun only. Some with a
horn for powder slung under the arm, and a few with old rusty,
mouldy cartouch boxes. Perhaps there was not a bright gun
in the whole regiment. Col. Hutchinson and Maj. Goodwin of

the cavalry came on, but as their troops did not appear, they were merely spectators. They both appear respectably, the former like a veteran the other like a daring, fierce, undaunted son of Mars. After the review and manoeuvering were over, the governor and his suit dismounted, left their horses, and walked up to meet half way the Field and Company officers in front of the line. The Gov. then made a very sensible and pertinent address to them; not an eulogy or a compliment: but he regretted the want of military spirit and discipline which he perceived, and told them in plain terms that both officers and soldiers were censurably deficient. He addressed them seriously on the consequences of the undisciplined state of their troops in case of a war, and urged several considerations to stimulate them to exertions; such as their proximity to the seat of government, where they would be more noticed by the public &c. Col. Meyer, in the midst of this censure, undertook to put in a word by way of apology. Gov. Hamilton took no other notice of him than to turn his eye and say " I'm not to be interrupted"—then went on with his address. The Gov. is a middle sized and middle aged man, has a handsome demeanor, speaks with some ease, but not with the fluency of an orator. * * * In short the whole business was ridiculous in the extreme and disgraceful to freemen. The troop of horse had no music, and in the Reg't of foot there were only 4 or 5 drummers and one fife and half of those were negroes. The companies were dismissed about three o'clock P. M. I did not see that rioting, drunkenness, fighting and general irregularity through the remainder of the day, which from the nature of the case, and the representations I have often heard made, I had reason to expect. Indeed I walked almost the length of the main street, towards night, to observe how it was; and found myself greatly disappointed. I saw some firing, and some clusters of men where there was a little high talk, but no quarreling, and indeed nothing more than what is frequent in the Northern States.

Wedn. Dec. 11th. A resolution passed in the Senate of this State today, to prohibit the freemen (or electors as they are termed) from voting in more than one place.[1] I understand that serious abuses of the right of suffrage have been heretofore committed by persons who owned property in different

----

[1] This resolution passed the house the next day ; Acts of 1805, p. 112.

districts and parishes, attending the elections in those differ-ent places, and exercising thereby an undue influence. By this means, the city of Charleston could gain an immense weight in the legislature: her citizens being accustomed to sally out and carry an election in several country parishes where the number of resident electors is small. The parish of St. Andrews is such an one: though containing only about fifty families, it sends three representatives and one senator to the General Assembly. In some parishes in the low country it is said the disproportion is still greater. The reason is, that the increase of wealth and the multiplication of negroes have diminished the white population. This was stated and explained by Simons and Alston in their speeches on the slave trade; thus: As one man grows wealthy and thereby increases his stock of negroes, he wants more land to employ them on: and being fully able, he bids a high price for his less opulent neighbor's plantation, who by selling advantageously here, can raise money enough to go into the back country, where he can be more on a level with the most forehanded, can get lands cheaper, and speculate or grow rich by industry as he pleases.

In the lower house, the bill for the abolition of the slave trade had a second reading, and was considered clause by clause. The minority appear chagrined that the bill meets with such encouragement, and they are constantly trying some side blow to defeat its object. It is worthy of remark that as a general rule, the members of the lower country have favored the prohibition, while those of the upper country have opposed it:—there are, however, exceptions both ways. Of those who were strenuous for the continuance of the abominable traffic it is strange that some were steady baptists, who least of all would be thought to favor slavery. The bill is almost entirely indebted for its progress thus far, to the patriotism, talents and highly honorable exertions of the Charleston Representation.

JOURNAL NO. 2. AT COLUMBIA, S. C.

Friday Dec. 13, 1805 After spending part of the day in the office went over to the State House. The second reading of the Bill on the Slave trade was attended to in the Senate. The bill having passed the lower house, the public feeling is excited about its event here. Mr. Smith, a lawyer from York District made a long and rather tedious speech of nearly two hours, against it. He is not fluent, nor does he use the hand

somest language, but he in the course of his argument, gets
out considerable that is to the purpose. Mr. Stark of this
place also spoke at some length in favor of the importation,
and to justify it, attempted to show, on the authority of some
English traveller whose book he brought in and quoted that
the common inhabitants of Russia, and other parts of Europe
are in an abject state, and even as badly treated by their
Superiors as our slaves are by their masters. He believed it,
he said, a piece of humanity to bring them from Africa, because,
there, when taken prisoners of war, they are sold and enslaved,
or else tortured and killed. Mr. Izard also spoke the second
time against the bill, and denied that the wars in Africa are
instigated by white people in order to get slaves. No, said he,
with emphasis, they are wars of fanaticism, wars arising on
account of religion and enthusiasm (which are always the most
bloody) and carried on by the Mahometans against the reli-
gions of all other persuasions in Africa. The question was
taken on the 2nd which is the most important clause, and carried by 16 against 15. There is still room, however, at the final
question, for the opposers of the bill who are a strong party,
to make further resistance and perhaps overthrow it.

Saturday Dec. 14. Wrote a letter in the morning: then went
to the State House and saw the ceremony of ratifying Acts;—
to do which the House of Representatives preceded by their
Speaker, walk into the Senate Chamber. Then, in presence of
both houses, the Secretary of State, assisted by the Clerk of
each house, affixes the great seal of the State to those bills
which have passed through the requisite stages in regular
course. The Speaker of each house next subscribes his name.
This being done and the records of the proceedings being read
by the Clerk of the Senate, the H. of Rep. retires in the same
order.

In the course of the day, the final vote was taken in the
Senate on the Bill for the abolition of the Slave trade. The
principal debate being already over, little was said on it today,
except by way of explanation: but the minds of the members
being made up, all waited with anxiety for the event. The
question was put by the President, and the Ayes and Noes
taken; during which a peculiar solemnity pervaded the Senate room. In favor of the bill appeared the President (Col.
Barnwell) and fourteen members. Against it were sixteen
members. Of course it was lost by a majority of one. Much

joy was manifested by many. Some of the Senators even rose
and reached across tables and over chairs to shake hands with
each other, and pass congratulations on the event, the very
moment it was ascertained. There was a great deal of smil-
ing and much complacency also in the countenances of many
of the members of the other house who had come in to be
spectators, and of the audience generally. Horrid exhibition
of Horrid Republicanism!

Sunday, Dec. 15. A riotous scene took place which made
considerable disturbance. The Speaker of the H. of R. is said
to have been a principal actor in it. He and several members
of both houses together with some others went through the
streets in high glee with a drum and fiddle; to *set the town to
rights* as they term it. They went to the lodgings of a number
of the members, and in case of their failing to rise and admit
them voluntarily, broke down the doors of their rooms. * * *

Tues. Dec. 17th. * * * Had considerable of a chat this
morning, with a Dr. Wilson one of the family boarders, who
is a member from one of the low country parishes; but who
by the plainness of his dress and manners seems more like
one of the Mountain Members. From some remarks that fell
from him, as well as from others with whom I have been in
company, I find it is here considered a great thing to get
in favor with the people, to acquire a kind of control over their
minds and be looked up to by them as a leader. Speaking of
the militia the Dr. said a military commission is a valuable
thing, because the holder of it has such an opportunity to gain
influence by being known to officers and soldiers! By a little
remissness in the enforcing of the law and especially in the
business of fines, he has a rare chance to gain favor. This, he
said is the reason why so many Colonels and Majors are in the
Legislature. Another man, and a man of influence too, conversing with me this evening on the different professions,
thought he should prefer that of the physician to Law, because
it is a popular profession and enables one to get acquainted
with people and ingratiate himself in their favor. So natural
it is for Carolinians to exhibit in their common conversation, their ruling passion, ambition. That lucrative and honorable places are a great object with the people, about here
cannot fail to be evident to any one who is present during the
session of the Assembly. Candidates for Sheriffalties, and
other offices crowd into town, and wait for whole weeks

together at a great expence till the result is known; and they often send letters to every member soliciting his vote and interest. * * *

Thurs. Dec. 19. The town is in considerable alarm this after-noon. A rumor that began to circulate before noon has now towards evening received some confirmation, that a scheme of insurrection has been formed among the negroes on the other side of the river, a few miles above this place, in conjunction with a party below. Their plan is said to be to assault Granby and then come up and burn Columbia; first taking possession of the arms and ammunition deposited in the State House.

5 o'clock P. M. Capt. Fausts artillery-men are collected making cartridges and preparing to defend the town. The alarm is increasing, and yet nobody seems to know the true state of the case, or whether there be really any serious danger.

9 o'clock All is bustle and agitation this evening. Arms have been dealing out to the militia and others. Some are mounted on horseback, armed, and some are patroling the streets on foot. The artillery-men have a field piece placed on the eminence in front of the State House and a fire built up in order to alarm the town in case of any emergency during the night. One negro who is suspected of being active in the plot has been committed to jail today, and the patroles have orders from the Gov. to take up every one seen out. One poor fellow, it is said, has just been shot dead by the patroles at the north end of the town, and several have been taken up. The town negroes are all in dreadful consternation about the event fearing I suppose that they shall perhaps be butchered by one party or the other in case their country brethren make the attempt.—Mrs. Chapman had occasion to send to the Bakers for bread at supper, and requested me to go with him as a protector. The innocent fellow, even then, was much afraid to venture into the streets; and kept so close behind me as to crowd upon me.

The Assembly have been sitting all this evening, and intend to finish all their business in order to adjourn finally.

Frid. Dec. 20. The night passed without any new alarm. The panic which seized some people is moderated, and all is quiet. Further news from above, however, proves that the alarm was not entirely causeless, but removes the dread of present danger; for whatever project the slaves may have

H. Doc. 353——56

formed, they are now so intimidated, that nothing is to be feared from them. The negro who was killed last evening was on horseback following, at no great distance, his master; and as they had been out of town and not heard of the alarm, paid no regard to the patrole when hailed by him. It is said the Jury called to sit on his body have brought in a verdict of wilful murder.

The members and other gentlemen are leaving town in great numbers this morning. Some in hacks, many in chairs, a few in Phaetons, and a few on horseback.

P. M. The town is mostly cleared of its company and is becoming quite still and calm. It is indeed a calm after a storm; and it is really pleasurable to have once more such a season of tranquility. * * *

Saturday Dec. 21. * * * A court of Magistrates has been sitting for the examination of two suspicious negroes. One of them is said to have confessed being engaged in a Scheme of insurrection to be put into execution at Christmas time. * * *

[From December 21, 1805, to January 3, 1806, Mr. Hooker was occupied in a journey to Beaufort and back to Columbia.]

Feb. 9th. * * * We met also in the street a number of new negroes, some of whom had been in the country long enough to talk intelligibly. Their likely looks induced us to enter in to a talk with them. One of them, a very bright, handsome, lively youth of about sixteen, could talk well. He told us the circumstances of his being caught and enslaved, with as much composure as he would any common occurrence, not seeming to think of the injustice of the thing, nor to speak of it with indignation. He said his father and mother lived in Gola,[1] and he liked to live there himself. His appearance was manly, genteel and graceful, and such as indicated his having been bred in style. He told us that his Pa (as he called his father) was a Captain. He spoke of his master and his work as though all were right, and seemed not to know he had a right to be any thing but a slave. Another of them had his upper teeth cut or filed into sharp points. He could not talk with us, but as far as we could learn, they were designed to fight with and possibly he belonged to a Cannibal tribe.

I heard a fact this evening worthy of note relative to the sale of offices. Mr. Taylor, the Clerk of the Court for this District, has lately bargained with a Mr. Guigniard for the

---

[1] Angola on the west coast of Africa.

sale of his office for the sum of eight hundred dollars. I had the account from Mr. Egan who, being a member from the District, recommended the appointment to the Governor before it can be made and who had already been applied to for such recommendation. The office is said to be worth twelve hundred a year. I have before heard of offices being bartered for. A person of my acquaintance agreed with a candidate for the Sheriffalty of Lexington to procure him a number of votes in the Legislature for the consideration of a pretty valuable silver watch. * * *

Feb. 16. I had been applied to some time ago by the Trustees of the Cambridge Academy,[1] through the medium of Mr. North, to take the charge of their Seminary, whenever they should be ready to revive and put it in operation (it having been for some years neglected): and wishing to be present at their meeting on Tuesday, I set out for that place this forenoon, brother J. accompanying me. Rode 25 miles to Williams' tavern. We met there with Cowles Mead Esq. who was on his way home to Augusta, from Federal city, whither he had been as a member of Congress; but his election was disputed and decided against.[2] His journey to the Capital, however has not been in vain: for he has had conferred upon him the secretaryship of the Mississippi territory.[3] He appears to be a young man of about thirty, of handsome talents. Converses with ease, fluency and propriety. Appears like a man of good moral and political principles, and exhibits in his conversation on political subjects a degree of candor not often discovered in politicians of this day. His deportment is genteel—but his style of appearance is plain. He travels in a sulkey—with one horse, unattended by a servant; and carries pistols. Mr. M. speaks highly of J. C. Smith of Conn.[4] and considers him a very useful member of Congress. Mr. B. Bidwell[5] he says is becoming conspicuous, and promises to be one of the most able men in the House. J. Randolph[6] he

---

[1] Cambridge was a local but not a legal designation for the village which grew up around Fort Ninety-six. For the failure of the attempt to make this its legal name, see anecdote of J. C. Calhoun's father, in O'Neall, II. 283. For a description of the place and a history of the college, see post, February 27 and August 16. The Cambridge Association was incorporated by the last legislature; Acts of 1805.

[2] See Clarke and Hall's Contested Elections, 157-165, Spaulding v. Mead; and American State Papers, XX, 431-436.

[3] January 20, 1806. Exec. Jour. Sen., II, 16.

[4] John Cotton Smith (1765-1845), member of Congress from Connecticut, 1801-1806, governor 1813-1818.

[5] Barnabas Bidwell of Massachusetts, member of Congress 1805-1807.

[6] John Randolph of Roanoke.

thinks is fast losing his influence, and is even thought by some
to be going over to the Federal side. He represents Mr. R. as
one who is fond of having his own opinion prevail and can't
endure to have it controverted. Mr. Wright of Maryland,[1] he
represents as a passionate man, whose furious zeal on party
subjects will always carry him to extremities, and prevent him
from effecting any object that he wishes. * * *

Feb. 25th. * * * The town of Cambridge is nothing more
than a snug little village of 15 or 20 houses and stores on the
top of a small hill called Cambridge Hill. There is an area in
the center of it, where stands an old brick Court House. At
a little distance down the hill is the jail,—both in a neglected
state. Just out of the village in a pleasant plain, quite retired
from noise, is a two story brick building, which was erected
for the President's House of the college; but which is now
designed by the Trustees for the Academy building itself. As
for the other college buildings, they were never any thing more
than mere log-studies, temporarily thrown up, till better ones
could be erected—and they are now in ruins. The Rev. Mr.
Springer[2] from Princeton College was at the head of it; and
under his direction the institution flourished. He was a presbyterian divine of great merit. * * * After him several
persons had the charge of the Seminary, but it flourished less,
and finally became quite neglected—in which state it has been
for several years past. Though called a College in the Statute
Book, yet no regular system of College education was ever
established and no degrees were ever conferred. The famous
Robert Goodloe Harper[3] was once a student, and afterwards
an assistant instructor here, pursuing at the same time the
study of the law. The Village has seven stores and three taverns. Its appearance is not at all flourishing; and it is said
to have been decaying, ever since the new judiciary arrangement, by which the courts were removed to Abbeville. The
present town has been built anew since the war: the old town
of Ninety Six (as it used to be called) having been destroyed
by the British.

March 14. Met with my old neighbor and fellow voyager J.
North of Farmington. Pleasant, facetious and good humored

[1] Robert Wright, Senator 1801-1806, member of Congress 1810-1817, 1821-1823.
[2] Rev. John Springer, Princeton 1775, tutor at Princeton 1775-1777, died 1793.
[3] Robert Goodloe Harper (1765-1825), Federalist member of Congress from South Carolina 1795-1801, is perhaps best known by his "Observations on the dispute between the
United States and France," printed in 1797. He was a Senator from Maryland from 1816

as usual. I find that a plain looking man whom I used to notice in the State House at Columbia, and of whom I made a memorandum in my journal of Nov. 23rd is a Col. Barkley Martin of a neighborhood just below here. Mr. L. assures me that he is an excellent man and a worthy member of the Baptist Church; and that his objection to voting the Chaplain a salary must have been an objection of religious principle, and not of infidelity, as I at the time supposed it might be. I recollect however, to have afterwards noticed the same man, uniformly attending the same Chaplain's preaching.

March 15. Finished the 1st vol. Blackstone, with Christian's notes.—The people about here talk a great deal about the famous Judge Burke,[1] who used to attend the Superior Court in Cambridge. He must by accounts have been a man of most singular humor: He was thought to be a good Judge of law, but so fond of fun, as to forget very often the awfulness of the place which he filled and turn the whole proceedings into a farce. He once pronounced sentence of death on a culprit and added at the close of it, *" but don't mind, my good fellow, it's only what we're all got to come to."* *" I hope, said one of the lawyers, your honor don't mean that we're all got to be hung."* *" No," replied the Judge, " but we're all got to die, and it doesn't make much difference how."* Somebody in a company where he was present was eulogizing some of the Carolina law characters. *Aye,* says Burke, in his dry Irish way, *Ye may talk as much as ye plaise of your Pinckney's for an argument and your Waties's for a special plea in bar; but 'fore G-d, for a Roman gladiator armed at all points, give me Pierpont Edwards.* He was fond of having lawyers come directly to the point and meet it with good common sense; and could not endure a parade of words about nothing, nor had he patience to listen to those subtle reasonings of some lawyers, which only seem to embarrass the jury, and render an intricate case additionally intricate. Gen. C. C. Pinckney[2] had been arguing before him a long time one day, when judge B. suddenly started from his seat, tucked up his robe, took his hat, and left the bench. The lawyer of course ceased, as usual in such cases. *" Go on"* Gen. *Pinckney, go on,* says the Judge, *you lore*

[1] Ædanus Burke (1743-1802) an Irishman, member of Congress, 1789-1791, was a common law judge from 1778 to 1799, and an equity judge from 1799 to 1802. His pamphlet against the Cincinnati is famous.

[2] Charles Cotesworth Pinckney (1746-1825), famous as envoy to France, 1796-1800, and as Federalist candidate for the Vice-Presidency in 1800 and for the Presidency in 1804 and 1808.

*to hear yourself talk. Meanwhile, I'll go out, and take a ———
and a peep at the Camel".* (a camel was at that moment exhibiting for a show, in front of the Court House, among the people). Hence, *"peeping at the camel"*, is to this day a bye word among the Carolina lawyers, for *going out on any occasion.*— He was a great enemy to everything like pomp, and though he would sometimes like the other Judges submit to be attended by a guard of constables, yet he was very apt to turn the thing into ridicule. Being once on the circuit and about to ride from one court to another, he was solicited by a company of horse that was out for exercise, to accept of them for an escort. After some excuses he consented. By the time he was ready it began to rain. Among the back country people, especially those who dont own a great coat it is not uncommon to wear a blanket and they sometimes cut a hole in the middle of it and put their head through for the sake of better protection from the rain. Burke in his tours among them, had seen this contrivance, and resolving on merriment, procured him a blanket and fixed in the same manner. The cavalry drew up at his door, received their charge and set off amidst an intolerable shower of rain, escorting towards the next county a thing which looked more like a Catawba Indian or even a baboon than a man of state. Mr. Burke was on very intimate terms with his brother Irishman, the Hon. O'brien Smith of the present Congress, and used often when going on the circuit, to send to Mr. Smith for a horse to ride. Smith in pleasantry once sent him a valuable Jack-ass; not dreaming however that the Judge would make use of it. It was all very well however. The Judge mounted his Jack and began the circuit, but before he proceeded far, bargained him away for a horse of not one third the value. After three or four weeks, he came home from court, and sent home his neighbor Smith's horse without any explanation. Smith soon came over to see what had become of his favorite Jack. The Judge's first salutation was: 'Fore G-d, Mr. Smith, I reckon you'll learn, by next court time, not to send your Judge an ass to ride upon. A new court district was once established near the upper part of the State in a wild region, and it fell to Judge Burke to attend the first court. Not finding the way easily, as he drew near to the place, he asked a man to get into his chair with him and show him:—As the request was rather too peremptory to suit the free spirits of the mountaineers, the fellow saucily

refused. But 'fore G–d. said Burke, then we'll see whether
the public interest must suffer for want of a pilot to the Judge,
and springing out withall, he grappled the fellow neck and
heels, laid him in his chair and forced him to point out the
way. When he returned he was asked by a brother Judge
how he liked the new county. Aye, says he, you sent me to
administer justice, not among citizens but among beasts of
prey. Their glaring eyeballs looked like vengeance and 'fore
G— it wasn't any respect for their Judge that prevented them
from coming at him; but it was this right hand, that ensured
his safety. * * *

Thurs. April 1. * * * Witnessed a little piece of the
Carolina policy in road and bridge matters. As long ago as
my first coming to Cambridge, and I don't know how much
longer, "*The Repairing of the Bridge over Henley Creek*" was
in an advertisement offered "*to be let to the lowest bidder.*"
Five or six planks would have made it passable, yet it remained
unrepaired and impassable till yesterday, although on the
public road to Augusta, and the creek being inconvenient for
fording. * * *

April 10. This being "*tax day*", a multitude of people flocked
into the village to pay their state taxes and also the direct tax
of the U. S. which was laid by President Adams' Administration,[1] but which was never before collected in this State. I
made particular enquiries about the reason of the delay, and
could not learn that it was owing to any public aversion to
the payment, but to several accidental circumstances, such as
the death of some, and the failure of other officers concerned
in the collection. This tax is laid on negro slaves as well as
other objects. While we were at the tea table conversing
about it, Mr. Lilly,[2] pointing to a boy that was waiting on the
tables, said, "*There's a fellow that escaped this tax, by not being
born so long ago as when it was laid.*" * * *

Sat. April 25. * * * Had the curiosity to attend Mag-
istrate's Court, as they are called, held at the Tavern of Squire
Lipscomb. They are usually held once a month, when all the
causes that have occurred are brought together and decided.
The justice and his constable prepared the proceedings, and
both attend court. The parties come forward and state their
own case, producing evidence to substantiate it. The justice

[1] Act of July 14, 1798.
[2] A Baptist minister with whom Mr. Hooker lived while at Cambridge.

then determines as he thinks equitable and right. There is very little form or ceremony about it, and attorneys never appear for the parties. * * *

Tues. April 29. Have noticed since my residence among the Carolinians, a great many peculiarities of phrase and pronunciation. Some of them are vulgarisms and some being a characteristic of their pursuits and manners are proper enough, and convey an idea with force. Thus sportsmen and from them the people at large have introduced in common use the word distance in form of an active verb. Example I shall wait for you only half an hour. Now return speedily; or, by —— you'll be *distanc'd.* The low country abounding with swamps, which often prove embarrassing to travellers, it has become common to say of one who has got into difficulty of any kind, He has got *swamp'd.* The Navigation term "*clear out*" is common and as often used, very expressive. Thus Mrs. L. the other day finding some of the negro children who had come into the piazza to play with the others, making an intolerable disturbance, stepped to the door and peremptorily ordered all hands to "*clear out.*" The little negroes understood the commands and knew that their playthings were all to be removed and their departure to be final. Waggoners speak of being stall'd, when their wheels have got into a mud-hole too fast for their horses to extricate the load: and hence the term is sometimes applied to other cases, as for example to a school-boy, who is perplexed by an intricate question in arithmetic. To tote a thing means to carry it on the head: but it is sometimes applied to any lifting. *Carry* a horse to water is vulgarly used for *lead him* to water. Crap for crop. Even sensible men speak of their crap of cotton and crap of tobacco. *Hauling* wood and *hauling* fodder &c. is in general use for *getting* or *waggoning* wood &c. Tackey is universally applied to a mean horse. By *filly* is meant a mare—more especially a young one. *Cabin* is used for a log house or any poor mansion. *Raly* for *really.* *So help me* is an expression put by those who are not quite profane enough to annex the name of Deity, at the end of an affirmation which they wish to strengthen. The use of the word *like* is peculiar: Eg he acts just like he would if he were crazy. Instead of saying, I rode a little farther, the Carolinian says, I rode a *piece* farther. *Too* is used for a superlative—Eg. What a fine girl Miss W. is! She is *too* handsome. *Clever* for likely, learned, able, excellent. *Mighty* is in everybody's mouth, for *very*—also *powerful* for *big* or *great*. *Very badly* is often used for *very much*: for which however, there is the authority of Horace: "*Cupis misere abire*". I *reckon* for I *believe*. *Cotch* for *caught* is very common. *Fotch* for *fetch* is in some use. *Yon* for *yonder*. *Good man* is often used for man of property, even without limiting the meaning to characteristic punctuality. "*All but*" is a favourite expression for almost Eg. We *all but* turned over. Did the horse throw him? *All but*. "*A heap*" is very awkwardly used in adverbial form for in a great degree. Thus: He likes it a heap.—"*Lie down*" is used for *going to bed* or retiring, and seems to be considered as a more refined phrase. The common introductory address to a Stranger is *Stranger*. Eg. Stranger, will you tell me which of these roads leads to Abbeville? For a term of calling, "*I say*" is usual. Thus, "*I say! Mr. H. are you going to the Post Office?*" When one calls loudly to another, the interjection O, is often inserted. Eg. Edmund! Edmund! O, Edmund! On the other hand, there are several expressions current among New Englanders, which appear equally odd to Carolinians: Such as a *stoop* for a *piazza*, a *stub* for a *stump;* a *keow* for a *cow;* *choars* for *little tasks*. Guess is a word, when used for believe, so confessedly Yankee-fied (as the Carolinians pretend) as to be made one principal criterion for determining who is a New Englander. * * *

Sat. May 23. * * * Capt. L.[1] was once a more public character than he is now, having been a member of the Legislature during the period which preceded the great change in politics throughout the Union. I suppose he was one of those influential citizens who were attached to Robert G. Harper,[2] and who did not afterwards join in the public denunciations against him. All who did not thus join were considered Federalists incorrigable—and to this day, in all electioneering campaigns throughout the old District of Ninety Six which Mr. Harper represented in Congress, there is no weapon with which a candidate can be more successfully annoyed by his opponent, than the public exhibition of him as "*one of Harper's men*." A mere Federalist is a *harmless creature*, compared with a Harperian Federalist.

[After this the writer was ill about a month.]

Wedn. July 2nd. * * * Great preparations are making for the celebration of Independence. The married gentlemen

---

[1] Livingston.   [2] See note on p. 884.

are to give a public dinner in the fields. I had quite a ceremonious invitation conveyed to me in a letter of the following
form and address:

Mr. Hooker—Presid't of the
    Cambridge Association College.

The Managers of a Barbacue given by the citizens of Cambridge and its
vicinity, present their compliments to Mr. Hooker—Requesting him to
favor them with his company on the fourth at Cambridge to participate
of said Barbacue with sd citizens in commemoration of the fourth of July.

> James Coleman.
> Joseph Griffin.
> Toliver Bostick.
> William A. Douglass. } Managers.
> Rich'd Ringold.
> Tho' B. Waller.
> James Bullock.

Frid. July 1. A very fine morning. We began the celebration of Independence, in the Carolina way, this morning, by
participating in a *flowing bowl* of Egg-Knogg, which Mrs L.
had prepared; and soon after breakfast returned to the village,
where, early in the day a large concourse of people was collected. About 11 o'c the three companies of cavalry, artillery
and Infantry were arranged and exercised by Brigade Major
Butler, and reviewed by Maj. Gen. Butler, of Edgefield.[1] He
appears pretty well on horseback, but exhibits far less dignity
on foot. His dress is very plain; and his appearance throughout is more like that of an old Warrior (as I suppose he is)
than of a mere parade officer. His rank in the militia is very
high having under his command half the militia of the State,
of which there are nine or ten brigades. He is at the same
time a member of Congress. I did not however, at the dinner,
when I was introduced to him, perceive in his honor any striking indications of greatness. He seems to be a man of sense
and information, but not much polished and improved by
education. The dinner was in a little thicket not far from the
village, and consisted chiefly of roast beef and pork—cooked
over fires that were kindled in a long trench dug in the ground,
about a foot deep. About 200 dined together. The tables
were served by negro slaves under the superintendence of the
managers. What an incongruity! An Independence dinner
for freemen and slaves to wait upon them. I couldn't keep
the thought out of my mind, the whole time I was there feast-
ing. Everything was well conducted except the toasts, the

---

[1] William Butler (1759-1821), major-general, member of Congress 1801-1813.

management of which was ridiculous enough. No notice was
given when they were commenced, and they were drank by
about a dozen at the head of the table, while the rest of the
company were, some of them, eating, others talking and laugh-
ing and others sauntering about, without knowing of any
toasts being drank, except by the sound of the cannon. Squire
Lipscomb presided; but was too modest and inexperienced
to keep the company attentive to what was going on. There
appeared to be no partyism in any thing connected with the
celebration.   *   *   *

Frid. Aug. 1. Fine weather, as usual of late. Called in as
I often do, and had some pleasant chat with Capt. Gowdy.
He is an old inhabitant here and almost the only native citizen
in the village or its neighborhood. He speaks highly of Col.
Cruger[1] the British Commander here while the fort was in the
possession of the enemy. Says he was a finished gentleman
in all his conduct and treated the inhabitants with much
civility, punishing his men for abuses committed and restoring
to the owners plundered property. Some of his under officers
were also civil—and all of them behaved with a gentleness
that was much to their credit, when compared with the inhu-
man rapacity of the tory inhabitants. The siege of Ninety
Six[2] is a favorite topic with the people in this vicinity. It is a
pleasure to witness the animation that sparkles in their countenances, when in compliance with my request, they narrate
the minute incidents of those trying times. Some of the striking particulars are these—the blockading of the British troops
in the fort—the extension of a mine under the British works—
the sallying out of a British force which in spite of a desperate
resistance drove the Carolinians from the mine and surprised
unawares the heroic fellows that were almost ready, under
ground, to blow the whole garrison to destruction—the marching up of a pick'd company of valiants to haul down with
hooks the bags of sand which lay on the top of the entrench-
ment, while muskets were incessantly blazing from behind
them—the act of a courageous tory who notwithstanding the
surrounding crowd of besiegers, galloped through and gained
admittance at the gate, with advices of an approaching
reinforcement.

Sat. Aug. 16. Warm but pleasant. Farenheit's Therm. 85°.
Spent the P. M. at Capt. Gowdy's in examining the old archives

---

[1] Col. John Harris Cruger, loyalist commander at Ninety-six.   [2] In June, 1781.

of Cambridge College. Found them quite interesting. Some of the first characters in the State were among the Trustees; but it seems there used to be great difficulty in getting the Board together; and also in collecting the monies subscribed. The institution was founded soon after the war, recd a college charter in 1785—began to decline about 89 or 90 and to have fallen into almost total neglect about 1795 or 6. Great sums were subscribed which were never paid. One or two of the subscriptions were one hundred guineas. Mr. Dessaussure of Charleston[1] appears to have made great exertions in favor of the Seminary. *   *   *

Tues. Sept. 2. *   *   * The people about here begin to feel quite interested in the Congressional election. Much electioneering is often used on these occasions. The following will suffice to shew what means are sometimes used and what kind of people the electors must (in considerable numbers) be, since such reports are capable of gaining credit. Gen. Casey[2] of Newbury, who represents this District is an old soldier, and a respectable, though not a great man. A report is now circulating that he is in favor of a speedy and universal emancipation of the slaves—that a bill for that purpose was rejected in Congress at the last Session by only a small majority, and that it is all important for slave holders therefore to withhold support from any man who is friendly to emancipation. A story was some years since circulated and believed that Mr. Hunter wished for a law obliging every man who owned fewer than 8 or 10 slaves and a certain quantity of land to give them up to those who had more. At the same time it was well known that Mr. Hunter[3] had not that number. Yet he lost his election and Robert G. Harper was sent in his place. *   *   *

Sept. 6th. *   *   * Muster day for the three militia companies: of course much company and noise in the village. Electioneering for Cong. and the State Legislature is going on rapidly in this district. A person told me he had seen letters from a person to several voters, announcing himself a candidate, and soliciting their patronage and influence. To such a height does the fondness for office and power rise. Malicious statements and letters to the injury of Col. Colhoun and Ezek. Colhoun are now in circulation— Col. C. is an elderly gentleman

[1] Henry William De Saussure (1763–1839), afterwards a chancellor from 1808 to 1837, and famous in that capacity.

[2] Levi Casey, member of Congress 1803–1807.

[3] John Hunter, member of Congress 1792–1795, Senator 1797–1798.

of much respectability and an elder in the Presbyterian Church
near Vienna—Now in the State Senate, but a candidate for
Cong. against Gen. Casey and Maj. Elmore. I hear a very
good account given of the Colhoun family generally, as being
firm friends to religion and good order. J. C. Calhoun[1] is a
nephew of this Col. C. and son to old Patrick Calhoun another
Presbyterian elder. The Rev. Mr. Waddel[2] is his brother in
law—Indeed he is surrounded by religious relations, who had
always calculated him for a minister and sent him to Yale
College with that view. *   *   *

[On September 15, 1806, the diarist set out with his friend the Rev. Mr.
Lilly for a tour of seventeen days, from Cambridge up into the Carolina
mountains and back.]

Tues. Sept. 16. *   *   * We stopped at Old Mrs. Maxwell's
a little beyond: *   *   * The family are of the most respectable class. Irish origin. Quite religious and of the Presbyterian denomination. House and furniture old and plain.
Everything exhibits the appearance of order and industry.
More books than usual on the shelves and these mostly religious. To this family belonged the Hon. Robert Maxwell,
once a State Senator and afterwards High Sheriff of Washington District; who was basely assassinated a few years since
by some of his ruffian enemies. The instigator, if not the
principal agent in the horrid deed was a Dr. Kennedy of Georgia, brother to the Kennedy who married Miss Baldwin of
New Haven. He was apprehended and imprisoned for trial,
but broke jail and escaped, was taken again, but rescued by a
band of desperadoes. Mrs. Maxwell, his mother, seems to be
much affected in speaking of the circumstances. *   *   *

Thurs. Sept. 18. *   *   * This part of the state,[3] is just now
in a state of some agitation, on account of the approaching elections. It is curious to see how high is the popular tone on all
such subjects.—A stranger would be led to think the fate of
the United States depended on the choice which these people
are about to make of Capt. Earle, or Col. Alston,[4] or Dr. Hunter for a Congressman, neither of whom, nor the people who
vote for them, are probably *valued a straw* at the seat of gov-

---

[1] John C. Calhoun was a college contemporary of Hooker's, graduating in the class above
him (1804). There is, unfortunately, no other reference to him in the diary. His uncle,
Col. Joseph Calhoun, was a member of Congress from 1807 to 1811.

[2] Rev. Moses Waddell prepared Calhoun for college.

[3] Near Pickensville.

[4] Elias Earle had represented this district in the Ninth Congress (1805-1807). Lemuel
J. Alston, successful in this canvass, represented it in the Tenth.

ernment. We met with one of them this forenoon, at a spring where we stopped to drink, and suspecting from his look and demeanor that he was some candidate for public favor, on an electioneering campaign, soon discovered that his name is Earle. He was very civil in recommending to us what parts of the mountain to visit as most interesting and informing us where we could find accommodations, guides &c. From Reid's we rode towards the mountains which for some time have been presenting to our view, their awful summits, in all the rude majesty of nature. We had not proceeded two miles, when we heard issuing from the thick woods that crowned the bank of Woolenoy river, the shrill-sounding voice of the mountain preacher. It was now the middle of the afternoon. The good people of Woolenoy Valley had assembled at their meeting house, for public worship. We drew near and listened. Rarely have I felt so pleasingly solemn emotions. The strangeness of the place—the shady gloom of the forest, heightened the contrast with the delights of a beautiful sunny afternoon—the sacred silence of the scene, as though the oaks themselves were listening to the preacher—joined to a sort of veneration for the character of these, simple honest, inoffensive and I hope religious mountaineers,—all conspired to raise my tone of present feeling far above the usual standard.—We alighted and went in. Our entrance caused some interruption. Several rose to give us seats—some offered to take our hats—and all stared at us. Mr. Lilly was recognized by some of the congregation. I heard their whispers. I can't think of his name said one—I've heard him speak, said another—Yes, rejoined a third, he's one of the first preachers in the country. I, on my part, wondered no less than they. The congregation was truly a novelty. I had heard of the simple manners of the mountain people, but I had not expected to find simplicity itself out-simplified. Many folks, I am sure, would censure their appearance, as indecent. The women were mostly without stockings and shoes; while a *shirt* and petticoat composed their whole dress: but some, in addition to these, had (I suppose, *by way of superfluity and set-off*) a handkerchief spread over their shoulders and a man's hat on the head. Their cloths however, as well as their persons, were, without exception clean and neat. The appearance of the men was also remarkably simple: but it struck me less disagreeably than that of the women. They too were mostly barefooted, and, (to use a common phraseology) in their shirt sleeves. The old adage, *as is the people, so is the priest*, was here exemplified; for Mr. Adams was likewise in his shirt sleeves. The sermon being ended, the preacher, who had perhaps seen Mr. L. before or else knew him by his dress and demeanor, to be a clerical brother,—observed that he was rejoiced to see in the house one of his brethren, from a distance, and should be glad if he would come up into the pulpit and add a word of exhortation to the people. Every eye was turned towards my friend, with eager expectation, when he rose from his seat, and modestly declined, alledging, by way of excuse, the fatigue of his journey. It pleased me much to see lying about the seats, a number of school books, but particularly Webster's Spelling Books. I could not have supposed before that they had found their way into these remote and obscure regions. After meeting, we accepted of a cordial invitation from Mr. Adams the preacher to ride home with him; he having, with some of his neighbors, promised to be our guide, tomorrow, in ascending Table Mountain. Crossing the Woolenoy, a few rods from the Church, we rode along the valley, parallel with the mountain range, about four miles and reached the humble mansion of the preacher an hour before sunset. It is on the most public road which leads through the valley—yet the road is very obscure, and the spot lonely. The house is a framed one—but has one story—comfortable size—furnished in a way and inhabited by a family exactly corresponding to the stile of the people, whose minister it belongs to. Our dinner was soon served up for us. It consisted of fresh pork and sweet potatoes cut up and set on in a large tin pan, without any bread or sauce, or any accompaniment, except salt. A chest not higher than our knees served for a table:—The end of another chest served for a seat for our kind host; while my fellow traveller and myself occupied the only chairs in the room. Having taken no food since morning our dinner relished well. We ate very heartily, and I have rarely perhaps never, made a meal with more satisfaction. After prayers, we retired early to a coarse but comfortable bed, which was furnished with curtains of a coarse sort of gauze.

Frid. Sept. 19. Mr. Adams is a young man of perhaps thirty two—not much improved by information—nor much acquainted with any books except the bible—but accustomed to hard labour for his subsistence. His wife appears also like a hard working woman—Both however, but especially the woman, are patient, obliging and hospitable to the last degree. They seem to estimate highly religion and religious people:—and they say they live among a religious community. Their proximity to the western country has probably tinctured the religion of these mountaineers—who speak with animation of the wonders that have been done and are doing in Tennessee and the back parts of North Carolina. We yesterday fell in company with two preachers, who were about crossing the mountain to attend a great Camp Meeting on Pigeon river—and who were quite solicitous that we should extend our journey a little and go with them. * * *

[The diarist and Mr. Lilly and Mr. Adams ascend Table Mountain, and return to the Woolenoy.]

Sun. Sept. 21. * * * During the service a little event happened, such as I am fond of noting, as exhibiting traits in the manners and character of the people. Two candidates for public favor who were out on an electioneering tour, came into the church attended by two or three others. One was Col. Alston of whom I had heard much in these parts, and who was exerting all his energies to get a seat in Congress; the other was a kind of understrapper to him by the name of Toliver, who was so modest as not to ask for any thing higher than a seat in the State legislature. They were returning from a Barbacue which Alston had yesterday given to the people on twelve-mile-Creek, and it having been last night announced that he would attend church here the expectation of the mountaineers was of course excited: for of the various candidates, he was one in whose favor they were considerably prejudiced. When he came in, all was attention. Men, women and children gazed as at some strange sight. From the Colonel's demeanor, a superficial observer would suppose he really came thither to worship God: but an adept in the science of human nature, would (if a Yankey) be apt to *guess* that he came to worship the people. He seemed to pay the strictest attention to the preacher, and to join fervently in the prayers; and after the hymn was read, he rose from his seat and joined in the singing; at which almost every other man in the house also rose, with an obsequiousness that disgusted me. Just before dismissing his congregation, I could not but smile to hear Mr. Dowther give notice "that *Old Father* Roper's funeral sermon would be preached" at a certain time and place. This plainness of speech is common to the Mountaineers, who often call one another of the same age by their christian names, and those who are older by the friendly appellation of father, uncle, or aunt.—A curious farce was played at the Church door after meeting. The candidates had stationed themselves conveniently, and were now very busy in saluting every man in the crowd, taking care to call by name as many as possible, and putting themselves on the terms of old acquaintance. Col. Alston was perfect master of the art, and played his game with so much adroitness as almost to persuade one that nobody could have a more cordial attachment to him, or feel a greater interest in his welfare:—but Toliver was much more awkward: and being necessitated to struggle against a more than ordinary share of clownish rusticity, he in attempting to be polite made most blundering work of it. Col Alston has seen Mr. Lilly formerly and was now quite exuberant in his attentions to him. Myself also he pretended to have seen at Cambridge—was overjoyed to meet with me now &c. &c. He might have seen me—perhaps passing in the street—or in some other situation; but confident I am that he never spoke to me—nor do I recollect ever hearing of such a man till within a short time. I presume it was merely a part of his electioneering system—or in plain terms a downright lie. His whole demeanor however was marked by such easy civility, as to gain the good will of all. He pressingly invited us to extend our journey into the District of Greenville, and to make his house our home for a few days. * * *

Mon. Sept. 22nd. * * * Approaching the village of Greenville, we pass in view of Chancellor Thomson's[1] beautiful seat—quite retired in the woods, about two miles from the Court House. Arrived at Col. Alston's about 12. His seat is without exception the most beautiful that I have seen in South Carolina. The mansion is on a commanding eminence which he calls *Prospect Hill*. Fronts the village of Greenville from which it is distant just six hundred yards; and to which there is a spacious and beautiful avenue leading formed by two rows of handsome sycamore trees planted twenty four feet apart—the avenue being 15 rods wide. In like manner another handsome avenue formed by cutting a passage through the woods leads from the north front of the house to the mountain

---

[1] Waddy Thompson, sr., a judge from 1805 to 1828.

road, about quarter of a mile in length. The cultivated
grounds lie partly on the borders of the great avenue leading
to the village and partly on the borders of Reedy river, south
and west of the House. * * * Col. A. is as liberal in
treating with liquors as any body, perhaps, yet not extrava-
gant. Not aiming to shew his liberality by having the wine
and brandy cover the table and floor in slops, nor leaving it
standing about open, but on leaving the drinking room to go
to dinner or elsewhere he carefully corks and sets up the
decanter and bottles in the sideboard, himself.—After dinner,
I took a pleasant walk to the village with Mr. Henderson, a
young lawyer, who is half brother to Col. Alston. Introduced there to G. W. Earle Esq. the Clerk of the Court, and
Capt. Cleveland, a merchant. The Court House is a decent
two story building. The jail is three stories, large and handsome. The situation and aspect of the village is quite pretty
and rural: the street covered with green grass and handsome
trees growing here and there—but there is a want of good
houses—the buildings being mostly of logs. About six dwelling houses, two or three shops and some other little buildings.
The place is thought by many to be as healthy as any part of
the United States. Not a seat of much business. The courts
sit but twice a year and often finish their session in two or
three days. Only one attorney, and law business dull. One
or two physicians in or near the village; but their practice is
mainly at the *Golden Grove*, a fertile but unhealthy settlement
ten miles below. One clergyman within six or seven miles
who preaches at the Court House once in three or four weeks.
On our return, at tea time, we found a young Mr. Cleveland
from Tugaloo settlement in Pendleton, and several others who
had met Col. Alston to consult about the Electioneering matters. A social company spent the evening here. It was somewhat amusing to hear the various conversation on such topics.
From what I have heard I learn that the great objections relied
on in the Electioneering war are that Hunter is so good a physician that he can't be spared long enough to go to Congress—
that Earle does not respect religion, for when he is on his electioneering campaigns instead of going into the church he stays
out in the Shade with such as choose to stay and drink with
him. and that Alston is a federalist and in favor of a stamp
act and too rich a man! Alston too lays great stress on the
objection that the others are not Speakers—and he tells a

story of their all three mounting a stump, and addressing a militia company a few days since at the request of the Captain who wished his soldiers to have an opportunity of judging on their respective merits. He at the same time repeats the speeches made by them severally, taking care to represent the others in a manner comical enough. The fact is Alston is flippant on every thing whether he understands it or not,—but unless he founds his seat in Congress on something better than his oratorical powers, he will have, I am sure, but little support from men of sense and discernment. * * *

Wedn. Sept. 24. * * * Henderson in the course of his pleasant chat related several anecdotes about his brother Alston's art in electioneering. Among other things he told me that the large family-bible which lies on the table in the keeping room was not bought till since he became a candidate for Congress, and was then got for the purpose of making a good impression on such as might call in. * * *

Thurs. Sept. 25. * * * Passed the time in a pleasant and instructive way. The general[1] converses with ease and perspicuity on all Congressional topics appears to possess much valuable information on the state of the country, and to be candid and independent—not a partisan, but acting from the result of his unbiased judgment. He is liberal in his sentiments—well versed in the knowledge of men and manners. Tall, stout, well built and of a military figure, quite grey and rather advanced in life. Perhaps sixty years old. He showed me a tolerable likeness of himself, done in gold leaf by Amos Doolittle of New Haven—and several painted likenesses of his Congressional friends. He related also many interesting and pleasant anecdotes of Congress men and measures. He is well acquainted with Duane, the editor, of the Aurora; and thinks him a man of the most extensive information he ever knew. He says that with those whom he knows perfectly, he is very intimate, but quite reserved in talking to one whose name and character he does not well know. Those well acquainted with Duane often go to him for information on Congressional topics and he is never at a loss to explain to them any point or else direct them to some book that will place the subject in a clear view. Duane has always made it an object to know and he does perfectly well know the name, character and residence of every man in the United States who is anything of a public man, and can give you almost any information respecting them.

[1] Gen. Thomas Moore, member of Congress 1801-1813, 1815-1817.

Gen. M. speaks highly of J. C. Smith of Conn. as a candid, well informed and great statesman and of Griswold as a financier—Mr Bidwell and Mr. Randolph also he considers men of talents. * * *[1]

Sat. Sept. 27. * * * We arrived at Greenville about 9 and after breakfast, rode to Pickensville 13 miles in company with Col. Alston and a young Mr. Lester. Forded the river Saluda in our way become by this time, a wide, but shallow, stream interrupted by rocks and considerably rapid. Arrived about noon. Quite a public day there. A regiment of cavalry paraded in the woods, made a martial appearance, but there was a coarseness and rusticity about them, characteristic of the country they inhabit. It is said the troops were called out in subserviency to electioneering purposes. Several hundreds of people came together: the houses and streets were thronged. The three candidates for Congress, Alston, Hunter and Earle were present electioneering with all their might—distributing whiskey, giving dinners, talking, and haranguing, their friends at the same time making similar exertions for them. Besides these, there was a number of Candidates for the Assembly. It was a singular scene of noise, blab and confusion. I placed myself on a flight of stairs where I could have a good view of the multitude, and there stood for some time an astonished spectator of a scene, the resemblance of which I had never before witnessed: a scene, ludicrous indeed when superficially observed, but a scene highly alarming, when viewed by one who considers at the same time what inroads are made upon the sacred right of suffrage. Handbills containing accusations of federalism against one, of abuse of public trust against another—of fraudulent speculations against a third—and numerous reports of a slanderous and scurrilous nature were freely circulated. Much drinking, swearing, cursing and threatening—but I saw no fighting. The minds of uninformed people were much agitated—and many well-meaning people were made to believe the national welfare was at stake and would be determined by the issue of this back-woods election. Dr. Hunter conducted with most dignity, or rather with the least indignity on this disgraceful occasion—confining himself to a room in the tavern, and not mixing with the multitude in the street—Alston fought for proselytes and adherents in the street: but took them into the

[1] John Cotton Smith, Roger Griswold, Barnabas Bidwell, John Randolph. See previous notes.

bar-room to treat them but Earle *who loved the people more than any of them*, had his grog bench in the middle of the street and presided over the whiskey jugs himself. Standing behind it like a shop boy behind his counter, and dealing out to any one who would honor him so much as to come up and partake of his *liberality*.

Earle is the present member. I wish it were possible for Dana[1] to see him in his present capacity, that he might give him a true send off at the seat of government, and sure I am that his honor Capt. Earle would have hereafter very little ambition to shew his head in Congress Hall. I was introduced to a number of Strangers on this occasion—among the rest to Chancellor Thomson and Mr. Andrew Pickens. The Chancellor is a sleek, beauish young man of about thirty—whose dress and general appearance as illy accorded with my notions of a Judge's gravity as the active part which he was taking in this electioneering squabble accorded with my notions of a Judge's impartiality. He treated me very politely and invited me to visit him at his house. Mr. Pickens is a worthy young gentleman of about twenty-six, son to old Gen. Pickens[2] who figured in the revolution. He graduated at R. I. College and has lately been admitted to the bar. He is respectable, well informed, has the character of being sternly virtuous, and upright—and is a man of abilities—but his mien is rather authoritative—and he is so independent in opinion as to appear somewhat dogmatic. I was gratified to meet with at least one man who came hither not to *gull* nor to be *gulled*, but like myself to observe mankind—and who could so readily and so feelingly deplore the abuses of freedom which it is becoming so common to commit. Towards night I left this scene of clamor and confusion and disgrace, which seemed likely to continue through the night, and rode nine or ten miles on my way to Pendleton. Very few houses on this road, and the land unpromising in appearance. Found good accomodations, at the house of Mr. Johnson, where I again met with Mr. Pickens. My host proved to be a worthy young man and in his and Mr. P.'s company I spent the evening agreeably.

Sun. Sept. 28th. * * * Rode on to Pendleton Court House before breakfast, leaving Mr. P. behind, having prom-

---

[1] Samuel W. Dana (1760-1830) member of Congress from Connecticut.

[2] General Andrew Pickens (1739-1817) was conspicuous for his services in the southern campaigns of the revolution. His son, Andrew Pickens, who was graduated at Rhode Island College in 1801, was governor of South Carolina, 1816 to 1818.

ised to meet him again at church today and thence accompany him home: for he had invited me to spend two or three days with him.   Pendleton village is pleasantly scattered over a cluster of little stony hills, and is laid out in four squares—has ten or twelve good houses (some of which are large and handsome) a strong stone goal, and an old Court House. * * * Mr. P. introduced me to his consort an accomplished young lady who is a step-daughter of the Rev. Mr. M'Elheny:—and agreeably to my engagement, I accompanied them home. They live in the old family mansion—the general his father having removed to a farm at the foot of the mountains 15 or 20 miles distant.   The house stands on a high and prominent bank of the river Seneca, w[h] after coming boldly up to the foot of the hill at the end of the house, turns suddenly back, and then circuiting round about half a mile in front of the house forms a large and beautiful tract of fertile low grounds in full view.   It was on this spot of intervale, that the famous treaty of Hopewell was formerly made between Gen. Pickens on the part of the State, and the powerful tribe of Cherokee Indians,[1]—The house is two stories high—has an oldish appearance—furniture decent not elegant—table well furnished—Mr. P. asks a blessing at table (sitting) with much decency—a practice more common than I feared it was for a considerable time after my coming into Carolina.   I observe it in many families of respectability in the upper country—even in those where no particular pretensions to religion are made. * * *

Mon. Sept. 29. * * * After breakfast Mrs. Pickens entertained me with a number of fine turns on her piano-forte, accompanied by her voice.   It was a species of entertainment that I had little expected to find among the *unrefined people of the upper country*, and therefore the pleasure was doubly exquisite.   Mrs. P. informs me there are two piano's besides her own, in Pendleton.   After this, rode with Mr. P. into his low grounds, and saw a beautiful meadow of red grass and white clover which every year affords him a great quantity of hay. About six acres of it.   It is the only meadows I have seen in South Carolina.   He is much like a New England farmer in having a large barn filled with hay and grain—in working oxen, in cultivating apple-trees, and he says he intends to get still more into that way, and to be less intent on cotton and other money-making crops. * * *

[1] Treaty of November 28, 1785, negotiated for the United States by Pickens and three others.

Wedn. Oct. 1, 1806. * * * I came home [to Cambridge] in excellent health and with a fine stock of good spirits—and I brought with me some corrected notions of the Mountain people, who have not unfrequently been represented as intolerably savage in their manners—I have met with as pleasing instances of genuine politeness and courtesy and behavior among them as in any country parts of the State: and I have reason to believe the proportion of well bred people near the mountains is as great as any where else. * * *

Wedn. Dec. 31. Met with 2 or 3 Kentucky horse drovers in the village and being anxious to learn the feelings of that class of people respecting Col. Burr's projects in the west, I easily scraped a sort of Yankey acquaintance with them. One of them who was just from Frankfort where some of the operations have lately undergone public scrutiny told me he thought Burr a d—d good fellow, and had many friends. Once said he I used to think him proud, but I am much disappointed and find him a clever, affable good natured fellow. * * *

[Having been called to a tutorship in the South Carolina College at Columbia, Hooker left Cambridge March 3, 1807, and on March 6 began his service as tutor.]

JOURNAL NO. 4.

Sat. April 18th [1807]. * * * The Ct. adjourned about ½ past 10. It appears to me that courts here are in a much greater habit of expediting business than in Conn: 2 juries being kept by here, that as soon as one case is submitted to one jury, and they have retired. another may be immediately begun with another jury. Sometimes the latter jury goes out before the other comes in: when the Judge improves the time in hearing motions and doing that kind of business which may be done without a jury.—Judge Trezevant[1] who held this court is extremely industrious and indefatigable.—He appears to be about 36 or 7 years old is very thin and reduced, low in health and been in a consumptive, declining way several years. Still he goes into court at 9 in the Morn'g. and sits frequently till 8 or 9 in the evening without leaving his seat more than once throughout the day: once this week and only once he discharged the court about an hour and half for dinner.—He is very rigid in adhering to the rules of Court and the general rules of law and will by no means vary from them without the

[1] Lewis C. Trezevant (1770-1808) judge from 1800 to 1808.

most extraordinary and forcible reasons: very precise too about order, not suffering any the least unnecessary noise: and often reprimanding the sheriff if he does not see order kept and decorum observed. His charges to the Jury are very short, clear and illustrative and usually given with an appearance of great impartiality. He is sometimes displeasing by being so authoritative: frequently stopping the attorneys and making them sit down or take a different course of argument. * * *

Sat. July 4th. * * * The exercises [in the college chapel] were the singing of one Ode, one psalm tune and 1 National song, a Prayer by President Maxey[1] and an oration by myself,—and they took up about an hour and half.—After meeting the several dining parties retired to their several retreats. A social party of between 20 and 30 citizens dined at Mr. Chapman's:—amongst whom were Col. Taylor, The Intendant and other town officers, the Pres. Profrs and Tutors of the College and several State officers, together with the sheriff and clerk of the District. Much harmony and good humor prevailed; The toasts were moral, patriotic, and free from party spirit.—There was one singular circumstance I observed in making out the toasts which might seem to denote an inconsistency in the republicanism of some people. The Hon. J. Taylor (a Mem. of Congress) The Treasurer and Surveyor General of the State together with myself were appointed a Committee by the Pres. of the Board to draw up a sett of Toasts. We all of us proposed such as occurred to us: and I after proposing several which were accepted, suggested the following viz:—"The principles of rational liberty—May the blissful period ere long arrive when they shall prevail throughout the habitable globe." I, in proposing it, had in view the other nations of the world in general, without once recollecting the circumstance of slavery in our own country. Taylor took it up and looking it over a little seemed at first to find no fault, but all at once spoke out; "O this will never do! Why 'twill include our cursed black ones." or words to that effect. I replied "Really I did not think of those in making out the sentiment. However I suppose there is none of us but would wish it to extend even to them at some period or other." Here all paused a little: When the Sur. Gen. said "I hope it may not be till we are gone." Says I, Well if the

---

[1] Jonathan Maxey: see note 5 on p. 847.

words " ere long" are objectionable we can omit them and substitute others. Taylor said the toast would not be an accepta-
ble one at the Table, so we concluded to drop it. * * *

Mon. July 6th. Very hot.—News arrived last night of the
insolent attack of the British frigate Leopard upon our Frigate Chesapeake.[1] Today the minds of people are greatly
roused and Col. Hampton has been about proposing to have a
meeting of the citizens on Wedn. to enter into some resolutions on the subject. * * *

Wedn. July 8th. Excessively hot.—A meeting of the citizens
of Columbia and some from Granby assembled at the State
House at 12 o'clock to consider the subject of a late British
aggression. But though a pretty large number flocked in at
first, there appeared to be a great degree of coolness and indifference, considering the serious nature of the subject; for
some soon went out before the business progressed and a great
many before it was finished; and little or nothing was said by
anybody. Mr. Stark went up into the Speaker's desk and
informed the people of the subject of the meeting and nominated Col. Taylor Chairman. Maj. Clifton was then nom[ted]
Sec[y] when after waiting a long time to get ink and paper, Mr.
Stark read the account of the Chesapeake and Leopard from
the Charleston Courier and then having made a very short
comment, nominated Mr. Wade Hampton, Mr. Nott[2] and Mr.
Thos Taylor a Committee to draw up a sett of resolutions
expressive of the sense of the meeting, and also an address to
to the Pres. of the U. S. A. * * *

Sat. July 11th. * * * Attended the town meeting at 11
o'clock where several resolutions were reported by the Committee and agreed to by the citizens after some debate. There
appeared to be more feeling and interest than in the last
meeting. * * *

Sun. August 9th. * * * Col. H. [Hampton] is now very
open in favor of what he calls "Hamilton's System"; viz an
energetic system. A large navy, display of power and conquest.
True says he to Brazier and myself A navy will cost money, but
we must make up for the expense by conquering some of the
W. India islands any one or two of which will bring us in wealth
enough in a year or two to pay for a navy. He would not con-
quer he says to admit them to equal rights with ourselves, but

[1] June 22. 1807.   [2] Abraham Nott (1767-1830), Yale College 1787, judge 1810-1830.

to "make slaves" of them. Colonize and make them productive of wealth. He acknowledges his opinions are directly opposed to what they once were, for he used to execrate Hamilton's politics and to start at the suggestion of any expensive measures:—Says he we have witnessed two glaring examples which make against our principles. Our principles that we have been contending for are Democracy or something as near to it as we can get. The first is that of the French people who by endeavoring to get a government of a popular kind have fallen into a cruel despotism. The next is that the majesty of our nation has been and may at any time be outrageously insulted by any little d—d British frigate and yet we can't help it. * * *

Thurs. Aug. 27th. Pleasant but warmer than of late. A military day and the town busy. A Company of Cavalry out and All the officers of the foot regiment. A good deal of drinking and some squabbling. 2 persons at Greens at Dinner were for hurling their chairs, knives &c at each other, but were prevented. The people about here seem very fond of being military characters, but still do not enter into the proper spirit of it. One man who has been Capt. of the troop and regularly resigned 2 or 3 years ago entered the same company again today as a private soldier. The Lt. Gov. of the State actually attended the meeting of the officers of the Regt today as a Capt. I am told, and does in fact command a company of common militia, in which there is not perhaps one man except officers equipped and uniformed. * * *

Thurs. Sept. 24th. Fine weather. Mr. Kennard tells me there are about 300 voters in the District (Richland) and among these he does not believe that there are 30 or at most 40 of them who are in tolerable circumstances (that is, with say, 100 acres of land and one negro to work on it) but on the contrary are very poor and very ignorant, generally lazy and often drunken. * * *

Frid. Oct. 2nd. Rather warm and foggy. Saw today a drove of 21 newly imported Africans pass by with 2 men who were on horse back. They were all dressed in red jackets and blue trowsers, and most of them walked Indian file. Poor fellows! they gazed about on the houses and people as they passed through the street, and did not seem to be dissatisfied. They did not know, I suppose, what they were coming to. Saw today an account of Y. Coll. Commencement. It seems there were 60 Bachelors and 25 masters one D. D. and one L. L. D.

Sat. Oct. 3rd. Cloudy and pleasant. Maj. Clifton had last week inserted in the papers a public notice headed with the words "Grand Parade"; ordering out his Battalion for military exercise: accordingly, 4 companies of infantry and one of artillery making about 160 or 70 men appeared before the State House at 10 o'clock. A number in every company were without guns, all were without bayonets and two-thirds without cartouch boxes. One company at first appeared to have only one officer and he had neither gun, sword, epaulette, boots nor anything more than a common overseer not even a military coat nor so much as a stick in his hand: After a while a Capt. came and exercised them from a "Steubens exercise" reading out the words with an affected drawling tone like an awkward schoolboy. However after the battalion was formed they appeared better than I expected and performed most of the evolutions, except marching, with tolerable propriety for this country. After a short intermission at noon, the Battalion was exercised an hour or so and then drawn up in a solid column to hear a spirited and truly military harangue from Maj. Clifton on the subject of the call from the President for a quota of militia. He exhorted them to be bold in their country's cause, to disdain a draft, and voluntarily offer their services to government. His address was about 8 or 10 minutes long: then giving them a minute or two to reflect on it, spread them out in a line and ordered the drums to beat along in front from one end of the Batt'n to the other. When every man, both officers and soldiers stept out 8 paces in front as a token of their offering (except 4 or 5 who as I afterwards heard were not enrolled members of the companies). The spectacle would have been truly pleasing if the men had all been equipt or even provided with guns only, but as many were not, it was so far too much of a burlesque on the thing to be entirely pleasing. There was a good deal of joy expressed and a number of cheers given by all the Batt" and spectators. After dismission, a number of persons, not obliged to do duty came up to the officers and offered their services also. Each of these was raised up on the shoulders of the crowd amid the huzzas of the multitude.—A good deal of noise lasted most of the night. * * *

Tues. Nov. 17th. Damp and rainy, cold and uncomfortable as yesterday. Four of us today sent in a written request to Judge Bay[1] to assign the law students a convenient seat in the Court

[1] Elihu Hall Bay (1754-1838), a judge from 1794 to 1838, and author of Bay's Reports.

Hall, which he did very readily and told the Sheriff to allow us to occupy the corner near the Judge's seat and at the end of the Jury's. The Judge got provoked at the talking and moving about in Court this forenoon and ordered the Sh'ff to take into custody whoever he should find talking. Rives went to the crowd near the door and brought up to the Judge a well dressed, civil man who had been talking lightly, and the Judge, after a severe reprimand ordered him to jail. At night application was made for his discharge but Bay would not grant it. I thought the whole looked like oppression and Mr. Scott said if a judge in Virginia should do so, he would be torn in pieces:—He said if he should send him to prison he would not hesitate to kill him, and, as it is, would call him a rascal, if it should come his way. He thought it sufficient ground for an impeachment.

Wedn. Nov. 18th. Cold, but clear and pleasant. This forenoon the man imprisoned for talking was brought into court and the Judge after another short lecture and admonition told him he might be at liberty on paying the jailor his fees.

JOURNAL NO. 5. S. CAR. COLLEGE.

Sun. Nov. 22nd. Fine day. Columbia now begins to assume a gay and lively appearance. Legislators, Lawyers and Judges begin to flock in. * * *

Frid. Nov. 27th. * * * Attended court in the A. M. and heard E. Pearson[1] examined for the bar. The Ex^n did not last more than 5 or 6 minutes. The questions were few and of a general nature, though various and unconnected. Such as "What are the great divisions of Law? Ans. Rights of Persons and Rights of Things. What are the foundations of actions? Ans. Torts and contracts. What is the first step in an action? Ans. Writ. 2nd.? Dec^n. Suppose a special plea is put in by Def. what must the P'ff do? Ans. Reply to it. What does our Municipal law consist of? Ans. Writ. and unwritten. What is the Written? Acts of Assembly and Congress. * * *

Frid. Dec. 4th. Very rainy and unpleasant. The legislature is at present very busy in the impeachment of a Col. Doyley of Charleston late Treasurer. The Senate forms the Court and sits with the chairs and tables turned round the contrary way from what is usual, and the members mostly wear hats. The four solicitors who are the Senate's advisers in matters of

---

[1] Philip Edward Pearson, afterward State solicitor.

law sit in their black gowns at a semicircular table near the President. The Managers on the part of the House of R. and the counsel for the respondent also wear gowns. The Managers are Mess. Gist, Simmons, and Drayton.[1] The Counsel Mess. Nott (from Connecticut) and Maj. Ch. Goodwin (from England). Nott has been speaking today two hours or more, principally on the law points which are involved. He contends that an impeachment must be brought while the officer is in power or not at all; and Col. D. has been out of office several years. He is accused of wasting or misapplying 10,000 dollars of the public treasure. * ˙ *

Mon. Dec. 7th. Commencement Day.—Weather delightful.

The exercises of the day began between 11 and 12 o'clock. The pieces were few but tolerably good. There were 5 regular graduates besides 2 Bachelors from Yale C. and 1 master, from Rh. Island College. The music was instrumental and very good; the performers being 4 or 5 of the best in the state. The degrees were conferred with considerable form. The President came down from the pulpit and addressed the Trustees briefly in Latin and introduced the candidates. Then took an arm-chair which stood a little forward on the stage and I took another Chair at his left-hand holding a handsome gilt duodecimo volume of French. They came on by 2 and 2. The Pres. addressed them in Latin sitting. Then presented the book; which they held while he said another sentence, and then returned to me. They being then Bachelors, the President rose from his seat and acknowledged them as such, in Latin. Then they retired and 2 others came on. The Pres't then pronounced *a degree conferred* on one of the class who was absent, and on one Master—a Mr. King of Darlington. He then went back to the pulpit and pronounced the Honorary degree of L.L. D. conferred on J. Drayton, Esq. of Charleston and D. D. on the Rev. Messrs Furman and Percy of Charleston, Waddel of Vienna and Alexander of York.[2] After this the graduates went out on the stage before the pulpit and the

---

[1] Keating L. Simons (1775-1819) and William Drayton (1776-1846), leaders of the Charleston bar.

[2] John Drayton (1766-1822) was governor of South Carolina, 1800-1802, 1808-1810, and author of a View of South Carolina and other books. Richard Furman (1755-1825) was for thirty-seven years minister of the First Baptist Church in Charleston. William Percy (1744-1819), an English clergyman of the Countess of Huntingdon's connexion, was assistant in St. Philip's and St. Michael's churches, Charleston, 1805-1819. Moses Waddell (1770-1840), a Presbyterian clergyman, brother-in-law of Calhoun, was at this time head of a famous classical school at Willington, near Vienna, S. C. Joseph Alexander (d. 1808) Princeton 1760, was a Presbyterian minister at Bullock's Creek, York County.

Pres. made them a handsome parting address of about 15 or 20 minutes. The Valedictory followed and music closed the exercises. * * *

Frid. Dec. 11th. Warm and pleasant. Attended the debates of the legislature in the P. M. Mr. Speaker Alston made an elegant speech of about ¾ hour in a Com. of the whole on the inequality of the representation. His speech was evidently a studied one, and in one or two places rather stiff, affected and unnatural. However, it was on the whole one of the most elegant things I ever heard in my life: the product of much reading and observation and exhibiting great fertility of imagination. * * *

Mon. Dec. 14th. * * * Then went to Mr. Chapman where I heard Governor Drayton play a few tunes admirably on the piano forte. Then went to the Representatives Chamber where I heard the Rev. Mr. Weems a famous preacher, author, book-seller &c.[1] preach an eloquent extempore sermon on **Love to neighbors** &c. He seemed to think love the sum and essence of Christianity, and this a physical affection, attainable by all. It is said he always preaches in the same strain.

Tues. Dec. 15th. Very warm. Was today introduced to Mr. Witherspoon, a pleasant mild-looking and polite member from Williamsburg—to Dr. Blythe of Georgetown and to Dr. Jameison of Orangeburg. The Senate yesterday rejected unanimously the Bill to vest the power of licenses &c. in the Trustees of Coll. also the Duelling Bill and the Equity Bill. How much time is lost in laboring business in one house for the other house to *knock up.* The Bill respecting licenses easily passed the H. of R. and was thought absolutely necessary to prevent dissipation among the Collegians. But the Senate is much weaker in talents and information than the House.

Wedn. Dec. 16th. Very pure and pleasant air.—A. M. attended the impeachment of Col. Doyley. * * *

Thurs. Dec. 17th. Fine weather.—This afternoon attended the impeachment. In the eve. attended the Senior Exhibition in the Chapel and after that went again to the State House and heard Mr. Drayton's closing argument on the part of the state against Doyley. He is a young man of perhaps 27 a soft mild speaker; somewhat flowery and pretty luminous. About half past 10 the Yeas and Nays were taken and he was found guilty unanimously on the first Article and by more than two

[1] The famous Mason L. Weems, author of the "cherry tree" life of Washington.

thirds of the Senators on the two others. The Senate then directed the Managers to inform their house of the result thus far; and deferred pronouncing sentence till the H. of R. should request it. * * *

Frid. Dec. 18th. Fine weather.—At 12 oc. the Senate at the request of the H. of R. pronounced sentence on Col D'Oyley. The H. of R. came in and stood round. The Clerk of Senate called each member of Sen. by name, and then each rose and gave his opinion of the punishment that ought to be inflicted, most of them at the same time laying their hand on their breast. The majority were for having him disqualified to hold any office of honor, trust or profit under the state for five years; which sentence was accordingly pronounced by Mr. Smith the President.[1] * * *

[During a college vacation the diarist made a short trip to Augusta, Ga.]

Thurs. Jan. 7th. [1808]. Some rain. Wet and cold uncomfortable weather. Sat an hour or so in the Treasury Office with Mr. Haile. Mr. H. says the Treas'r is obliged to give bond for about 30,000 Dollars; and yet there is often in the Treas'y 40 or 50 and sometimes 60,000 Dollars.—He says the taxes from the Upper Division do not bring in so much as this Treasury is called to pay out, by considerable and he is obliged to bring up money from the Charleston Treasury.[2] * * *

Tues. March 22nd. * * * At 4 o'clock rode out with Brother J. and returning we agreed to reckon up the number of dwelling houses in Columbia;—calling those dwelling houses which families reside in or designed for such use. So we rode through Richardson and two or three other streets and counted them. The result was one hundred and twelve: viz on Richardson or the Main street 52. On the different streets east of Main street 46. On the streets west, or between the Main street and river 19. I suppose about five or six new ones are building which we did not count. * * *

Mon. April 18th. Very clear and cold. Otherwise fine weather. Attended Court today. Judge Wilds[3] presided. He is quite young; I believe 32 or 3; but yet has a good deal of dignity and is notwithstand[ing] very conciliating. The

---

[1] William Smith.

[2] The State had two treasuries, one at Charleston, one at Columbia. In the year October 1, 1806–October 1, 1807, the low-country treasurer took in $441,725 and paid out $307,660, while the upper-country treasurer took in $69,523 and paid out $68,918. Report in Acts of 1807.

[3] Samuel Wilds (1775–1810), judge since 1804.

juries at this Court both grand and petit, were I think composed of more enlightened men than I have ever seen them before. The Foreman of the Grand Jury was John G. Guignard Esq. The Foreman of 1 pet. jury was Dan'l Faust Esq. Of the other Col. W. Hampton. I am told he said today it was the first time he ever served on a jury in his life. The lawyers who spoke today were Egan, Hooker, Stark and Clifton. Egan appeared better than ever to me. He is really a Rhetorician. He is figurative and he shews the Scholar. His delivery is easy and his words mellifluent. * * *

NO. 9. JOURNAL. S. C. COLLEGE.

Sunday Nov. 13th. * * * F.[1] tells me that Mr. Cheves[2] an eminent lawyer and legislator of Charleston (now about 30 years old) was never blest with advantages of education and only went to a womans school a few months, until when past 20 he went to somebody a little while to assist him in learning Mathematics, but was a mere shop boy in his father's shop in King street, but having got some taste for reading he resolved to study law, and set in. Afterwards he learned other things and now can comment with propriety upon many of the Classics, understands Math. and Nat. Phil. is an admirable logician and excellent moralist. * * *

[Being called to a tutorship in Yale College, Mr. Hooker had resigned his position at Columbia. On November 23, 1808, he set out for New Haven.]

Tues. Nov. 29th. * * * About Cape Fear river I understand that people are mostly Presbyterians. On the creeks along this Side and towards Raleigh, the Baptists are most numerous. About Raleigh there are a good many Methodists. Most of the people on this road seem much to dislike the Embargo and say it is "ruination." They raise but little cotton. Those near the river make considerable tar and pitch, boards, staves and shingles to carry down. I saw about 40 barrels of tar lying on the bank of C. Fear river. They raise some tobacco also, but generally the land is quite too poor to enrich the people. Even on the rivers of these parts there are not such rich and extensive bottoms as on the S. Car. rivers.— After breakfast rode on (in the rain mostly) fifteen miles to Raleigh and stopped at Peter Casso's near the State House

---

[1] J. M. Felder of Orangeburg, a former fellow-student of the diarist.
[2] Langdon Cheves (1776-1857), afterward eminent as a Congressman and as president of the Bank of the United States.

about three o'clock. Warmed, drank some Apple brandy and immediately sat down to a various dinner but ate only Chicken pye, sweet potatoe pye and drank some excellent cyder.—Raleigh looks very neat and pretty as you enter it from the South. Mostly on one wide street. Houses generally small, neat and white, though there are a number of little ordinary rough unpainted shops and cabins. There may be fifty houses and stores. The State House is a very handsome building, far superior to that of the South State. It stands in the centre of the street in a large open Square of many acres with beautiful copses of pine and other trees which give the place a very rural, charming appearance. The edifice is of brick, painted and pencilled. 2 large stories high Square but parallelogrammic: 9 windows in length and about 3 in breadth: a door and small piazza on each of the four Sides—the lower part open except the corners where are offices.[1] The houses, as houses had adjourned, but each house was doing business in the Committee way. The Repr^s were engaged in considering petitions for divorces. I was astonished to see how lightly they regarded the subject. One was a petition for Divorce from the Man and Wife both. The argument for it was, that the leg. some years ago had allowed them to divide the property and now their happiness would be promoted by dissolution of the contract. One member said the Man lived in habits of adultery and perhaps the woman too might follow wrong habits. Both could marry to suit their minds and it was better then to do away their offenses by divorcing and permitting them to marry. They did not seem to investigate subjects deeply nor enter into the spirit and true principles of the case. Recruiting advances tolerably here. About 30 have enlisted. Two or three papers are printed here. One (The Star) a literary paper of some merit. In a piece on the lit. character of N. Car. four names are mentioned as models of American genius and talents viz: Rush, Dwite, Henry and another perhaps [Barlow] Washington.[2] It was written by an observing foreigner. He says that the Pres. of the N. C. Univ. is a man of talents, but as little animation and energy as he ever witnessed. The Academies with few exceptions have illiterate teachers and the reason is that here, as

---

[1] A picture of this State House may be seen in the American Historical Register for May, 1897, p. 183.

[2] The name of Barlow is erased in the MS., and that of Washington written above.

well as in all the States, men engaged in the business of education are not liberally compensated. There is said to be a good Academy in this town. Some embroidery work of a pretty neat style over Casso's fireplace denotes also that the education of young ladies is not neglected. * * *

Wedn. Nov. 30th. * * * Soon after my arrival[1] I sent my name to Mr. M. Dickinson[2] the principal of the Academy, who graduated at Yale one year before me. Dickinson soon came, took tea with me at Hill's. Spent 2 or 3 hours pleasantly; when we walked to his academy, a pleasant building on the hill about ¼ m. from the Village of Louisburg. We staid at his room about an hour, drank porter, read, talked and walked back to Hill's. L. is in a hilly part of the country has perhaps a dozen houses and 2 or 3 stores and mills on Tar river about as large as Farmington R. The shire town of Franklin Co. The County was named after Dr. F. and the village after Louis XVI at the time Dr. F. as our agent in the revolution went to F. and obtained supplies from the French. The river was thought (and still is thought by Mr. Dickinson) capable of being rendered navigable up here for boats at the time the town was built. The ground being hilly and the current bold, it would suit well for manufactures. Neuse River which I crossed about 12 or 15 miles back is a much larger stream. The Tar is navigable to Tarborough 50 m. below this. From 10 m. beyond Raleigh and onward this way the soil is more stony, the roads less even and the land better, though the greatest part is still barren. Old worn-out fields in abundance present a dreary decaying aspect. Mr. D. has acquired a very decent little estate since he first came here 4 years ago. He thinks himself worth between six and seven thousand dollars. The first year he had about seven hundred dollars—the next, the avails of his school 1000 Dlls—the next they amounted to 1500 and the last year to 1200. Besides this too he pays an Usher (Mayhew from Wms Col.)[3] 300 Dlls. But he has improved opportunities to speculate by lending say 600 Dlls cash to a young Sportsman and taking a Bond for 1000. Till lately he owned a house and farm of more than three hundred acres, six slaves, and a quantity of stock, as horses, sheep and cattle. Lately he sold his land for 4000 Dlls which was one thousand more than it cost him. He now keeps a Gig, two horses and a servant or two and designs in

---

[1] At Louisburg, 32 miles from Raleigh.
[2] Matthew Dickinson, Yale College 1804, died 1809.
[3] Davis H. Mayhew (1783-1822), Williams College 1805.

the spring to visit Conn *in this style.* Dickinson says literature is much respected in these parts and literary men reverenced. The first year he came when he had no property and nothing to recommend him but his books and his education, he received flattering testimonies of respect and was treated with equal civility as at present. When in Raleigh Gov. Turner[1] sent him a polite note inviting him to dinner with the British Consul, the Judge of the Fed. C. and several characters of eminence to all of whom he was introduced and by all of whom treated with respect. He says men of information and liberality respect literary men from principle and the rest of the community see in literary characters something so superior to themselves that they are impelled to homage. D. has had at times 90 students in his Academy. 20 or 30 or more as large and as old as himself. 20 once came at a time from the Univ. of N. C. having conceived disgust at the Monitorial law, imposing an oath on all by turns to act the part of spies on each other's conduct. He has taught all branches taught in colleges, except Conick Sec^ns. As to the learned professions, here in the middle country Mr. D. speaks thus. That of Theology is at low ebb, there being no preachers of education. He has never seen one Pres^n clergyman in the state except Mr. Caldwell P. of N. C. Univ^y.[2] All are Baptists and Methodists and very unlearned and in low estimation in Soc^y although perhaps very good men. There are many professors of religion, though mostly in humble life. There are however some exceptions. Some rich and honorable Sincere Christians, down below Louisburg. A wide field is open for the production of good by enlightened clergymen. In the law, there are some brilliant characters of education: Some good lawyers of superficial and limited educations, who appear very well but whose want of depth is discoverable to minute observers. Many mere pettifoggers who don't appear to any advantage. Many of the lawyers have been through a Latin course as they term it, i. e., as much latin as is read at Coll., have studied geography, Eng. G. Arithmetic and perhaps paid some attention to Rhetoric. and may be a little to Logic and then turned into the Law. In N. C. there are some very thorough bred and able physicians, especially in the Low country. But the greatest part are without good educations and many

---

[1] James Turner (1766-1824), governor of North Carolina 1802-1805, United States Senator 1805-1816.

[2] Dr. Joseph Caldwell (1775-1835), Princeton 1791.

are mere quacks. It is a common thing after reading a little latin and a few other things to go to Phil. a winter or two and then enter the practice. The education of ladies is not neglected. Good academies for them are in Salem, Raleigh, Warrenton and some other places. Mr. D. thinks the women have much quickness of apprehension and when refined by education as many of them in wealthy families, now a days are, they appear very advantageously. About Louisburg are many young ladies, *who touch the lyre most charmingly.* They understand music, painting and embroidery. Many young ladies from N. C. are sent to Bethlehem in Penn. and some to the Seaport towns.—I enquired of Mr. D. and Mr. Hill about the State of the University. Mr. H. gave me this Statement. The Legislature in former times invested it with all the escheated property of the State. A small part of it only was appropriated by the Board of Trustees. A few years ago the Pres. the Professors and the Tutors were Federalists. The first graduates for 2 or 3 years (at the least the likeliest scholars of them) were likewise federalists. In a short course of time a number of these graduates obtained seats in the Legislature and discovered talents that the rude, illiterate mass of old members either envied or feared. Under the ostensible motive of discouraging Federalism in the College (but really as Mr. H. says for fear of losing their influence in the Leg⁺ⁿ) these old members carried a measure for taking away from the Univ. all the escheated property that had not yet been appropriated. For two or three years this was a subject of altercation in the Leg⁺ⁿ till finally about two or three years ago, the good sense of a part triumphed over the prejudices of the rest and got the law repealed which took away the property; so that now it is the truth that the institution does possess it.—But the best property it has consists in donation of individuals. One citizen [1] left by will 50,000 acres of good land in Tenessee. This might be rented, but not sold till 3 or 4 years after his death, when the Trustees might, if they should see fit, sell one-third. Afterwards another third and so on. Not being settled it brought nothing by rent: Soon it may be sold, or perhaps is, in part and will therefore be of great Service. At present the Coll. has a Pres. one Prof. one Tutor.[2] Students

---

[1] Gov. Benjamin Smith (1756–1826), by gift in 1789, not by will: 20,000 acres, it is generally said.

[2] Dr. Joseph Caldwell, Professor Andrew Rhea, Gavin Hogg.

about 40. It is patronized by the State. The Pres. has other support than the tuition money. * * *

Thurs. Dec. 1st. * * * In this[1] county lives Mr. Macon[2] (pronounced here Meeken) a member of cong. and quite a favourite of this people. Also (in Warrenton Village) Senator Turner, formerly Gov. of N. C., and Judge Hall of the Sup. Court and Judge Baker. It is a very respectable, well informed county and has produced a number of eminent characters. There is at W. and for a long time has been one of the most flourishing Academies in the State. Warrenton is 55 m. from Raleigh, 25 from Louisburg and 85 from Petersburg (Vir.). The people in these parts trade almost entirely with Petersburg; of course the Virginians have many debts here. Now sales by Ex" are suspended in V. the Virginians push for their debts here and very much worry the N. Carolinians, who want such a law here to protect them. Gov. Wms.[3] thought it improper to call the Leg" for that purpose last summer although petitioned to do it, by many. His refusal gave offence and a few days ago the Leg" removed him and elected Judge Stone. A year ago they removed Gov. Alexander of Mecklenburg[4] and put in Wms. * * *

Mon. Dec. 5th. * * * R.[5] appears beautifully as you approach and view it from the Hills a mile distant. The Capitol towers preeminent and appears gigantic indeed among the other buildings. The side of the Hill from the river up to the top seems covered with clusters of buildings—Remote from the centre on the right and left a mile or two and at still greater distances handsome seats crown the top and sides of the mountain scattered here and there. Above you hear the roaring of the waters and see its white sheets here and there between the rocks and islands. Below a calmer scene invites you to look at the shipping which lies clustered in a bason or bend of the river. As you come up you pass through Manchester, a separate corporation on this side the river. Then crossing the very long toll bridge at the foot of the falls you enter one of the most beautiful cities on the continent. R. as I viewed it a mile or two off appears more like some of the drafts of European cities, particularly those on the Banks of the Rhine than any I had

[1] Warren.
[2] Nathaniel Macon, Congressman, Speaker, Senator.
[3] Benjamin Williams (1754-1814), governor 1799-1802, 1807-1808.
[4] Dr. Nathaniel Alexander (1756-1808), governor 1805-1807.
[5] Richmond, Va.

ever seen. Walked up a very steep hill indeed and visited the Capitol soon after my arrival. The House of Delegates had just met, chosen Mr. Hugh Nelson of Albemarle[1] their Speaker and were proceeding to Business. It seemed the most dignified body I ever beheld. The room was spacious and very elegant. The members in elliptical seats and around the Speakers chair. All with very few exceptions were well dressed and easy and graceful in deportment. Many young, mostly middle-aged and few or none quite old. Many spoke shortly and with ease grace and composure on the returns of elections from Amherst Co. Adj'd about one. Visited the Fed. Court with Micah Goodwin of Columbia, S. C. whom Capt. Scott found for me in the Capitol. Judge Marshall Ch. J. of the U. S. a most venerable looking personage of about 50 presided. Heard Mr. Wickham (one of Burr's counsel) speak in rather a colloquial discussion with the Ch. J. Saw Mr. Wirt, the famous orator in Col. Burr's case. A most beautiful, fair, elegant man of apparently 32. He is the reputed illegitimate son of old Peter Carns of Georgia and " *unquestionably the author of the letters called the British Spy*" as people here think. Ed. Randolph was here too—older than any, more plain in dress and somewhat venerable.[2] Gen. Mason perhaps one of Washington's Aids. Visited the Arsenal; a stupendous work indeed! Straight with the street in front and 2 stories high. A tower in the middle and at the ends. Circular in the rear. Saw some elegant Cannon and Bombs. Some of the Brass Cannon were French and German and Swiss 32 pounders, perhaps 10 or 12 f. long and weighing it is said 10,000 lbs, requiring 10 lbs powder. About 70 men only are now employed here. It is a state institution but far superior in extent and elegance to the U. S. Arsenal at Harper's Ferry. Thence visited the Penitentiary and was politely waited on around all its parts by Mr. Carter a very decent young gentleman employed there. The Criminals are 126—of various trades especially iron and leather. The guards are A Corporal and 6 privates at 6 Dlls per month. The Building presents a straight front with a central tower and wings of a towering kind terminating behind in a Semicircle. 3 stories high—The 2 lower ones workshops—the upper ones, places of confinement at night.—6 or 8 often work and

---

[1] Hugh Nelson (1768–1836), member of Congress 1811–1823, minister to Spain 1823–1824.
[2] John Wickham, William Wirt. Peter Carnes of the South Carolina and Georgia bar, Edmund Randolph, formerly Secretary of State.

sleep together without being fettered. They are not so rigor-
ously restrained as at the Pen^y of Conn. Punishments are
whipping or Solitary Confinement at the discretion of the
Keeper. Visited the Canal and the beautiful bason that it
terminates in, of 4 or five acres.—Here the Upper Country
boats come and land their cargoes; there are no locks to let
them down lower. Much coal is brought down from 12 or 14
m. above. It is the only fuel used in the city. * * *

Thurs. Dec. 8th. * * * Saw here [1] Mr. Winston a young
lawyer who resides at Hanover C. H., who had just come from
Mount Vernon 9 m. distant, and told me it was only 2 or 3 m.
out of the way in going to Alexandria:—So I resolved to go
round that way and improve the only probable opportunity in
my life to see the mansion where resided and the tomb where
lies the Saviour of my country:—but not being acquainted and
having no letters of introduction to Judge Washington [2] I
hesitated. Mr. Winston said it was very usual, he believed,
for strangers to visit the place although similarly situated;
that Judge W. was very complaisant and glad to treat them
civilly. About 3 m. from Colchester, which is a small mean
village, I turned off to the right, passed Gardners Mill 3
miles—Lewis' mill which belongs to the Vernon estate 1 m.
and going on about 3 m. came in view of the Venerable Structure where our hero lived, flourished and died. My emotions
in approaching the spot were singular. Here thought I, the
greatest man the world ever saw often rode out to view his
fields, visit the neighboring country and enjoy the beauties of
nature. About ¼ mile from the mansion you enter a gate, pass
through a pleasant grove of small, neat, well-trimmed oaks,
follow the path in some parts straight in others winding among
hills, at length ascend a tolerably steep hill and are present at
the house. I told a servant to inform his master that a
Stranger at the door wished to speak with him. Judge W. a
slim, neat, sprightly man of about 40 came to the door. I told
my name, object &c. and apologized for the intrusion. He, all
politeness and civility, instantly made me easy on that score,
begged to alight—asked me if I had dined—ordered a dinner—
called for wine and shewed me every mark of attention. After
sitting a few minutes and being introduced to two gentlemen

---

[1] At Colchester, Va.

[2] Bushrod Washington (1762-1829), associate justice of the Supreme Court of the United
States 1798-1829.

who were playing backgammon by the fire, I requested to visit
the domains. The Judge directed me to the gardens and the
German gardener accompanied me through the 2 gardens to
the Green Room &c., and to various places. Among others
to the Vault where the general lies and to the new Vault
where it is designed to have his corpse deposited. After looking round about ½ hour I came to the "long and lofty portico
where oft the hero walked in all his glory" and with a tele-
scope had a fine view of the Majestic Potomak—fort War-
burton—the shipping &c. &c. When Judge Washington
requested me to step in and take dinner. I did so and soon
after mounted my horse and rode to Alexandria (16 m. from
Colchester on the stage road and 19 this way) though very
politely invited several times to tarry all night. In short
Judge W. behaved very prettily and very genteelly. Easy
and graceful in demeanor, not affected, but takes pleasure in
pleasing others and making them happy. The Judge begged
me to "make his best respects to Dr. Dwight"—said he knew
him well and had a high regard for him. He has heard of me,
it seems,—for when I mentioned to him that I had a brother
in S. Carolina he asked me if my brother was not in the College at Columbia. * * *

Frid. Dec. 9th. * * * Crossed the creek which divides
G. T.[1] from Washington and rode to Mr. O'Neal's boarding
house where I took lodgings for a few days. About 11 o'c
after changing my clothes I walked 1½ mile to the Capitol and
with Mr. O'Neal entered the gallery of the Representatives
Hall a most Superb room in the left wing of the Capitol,
where a debate was proceeding on the Subject of empowering
the Pres. to arm and equip 12 new revenue cutters. Mr.
Blackley[2] was speaking at some length—pretty sensible, plain
speaker, though from Some defect in voice or fault in the
Structure of the room I could not hear him distinctly. Mr.
Sloan,[3] a very droll looking old man of quakerish principles,
dress and manners spoke a few words. He far exceeded my
expectations,—loud, clear voice—language tolerably correct
but very plain,—pronunciation rather vulgar, though not
worse than many men's—pretty good common sense. The first
resolution of a set of resolutions relative to our foreign relations next came on viz, that the U. S. cant consistently sub-

---

[1] Georgetown.
[2] William Blackledge of North Carolina.
[3] James Sloan of New Jersey.

mit to the late edicts of G. B.—In this discussion the merits and
demerits of the Embargo were introduced. Mr. D. R. Williams[1]
of S. C. made a long harangue of 2 hours upon it—justifying
the imposition and continuance of the Em^go. He recurred
much to his notes,—hesitated some—drank water frequently.
Began some sonorous and musical sentences which did not
close equally well. Began some so long as to lose the connection of words and make bad grammar,—but nevertheless had
a pretty eloquent speech and highly figurative language—
expressed very fair, liberal, national and harmonious sentiments—expressed himself in many instances in very strong,
emphatic language, and was by many people much compli-
mented and much admired. I think though, he was hardly
logical enough and rather too ungrammatical and incorrect to
pass for a complete scholar. For "effect an insurance" he
said "infect an insurance"—and committed a few other errors.
The Rev. Mr. Culpepper[2] of N. C. spoke ½ hour, plain man—
but tolerably sensible—very far from ornamental language and
frequently incorrect in grammar and pronunciation—Mr. Key[3]
(of Mar.) spoke 2 or 3 min. rather by way of reply—a very
sweet, mellifluous speaker. He showed the scholar and the
graceful orator. Mr. Newton of Vir.[4] spoke tolerably well
today, though very briefly. The House adj^d about 3. At 4
o'c we dined at O'Neals and rose about sunset. Several Southern members of wealth board here and yet are very temperate
drinking no wine and very little or no spirits and sitting at
table only about an hour. The dinner was a good one but not
splendid.—Ham, Turkey, Chicken, roast beef, chicken pye,
pudding, crackers and apples. Gen. Sumter, Gov. Milledge
and Gen. Trigg of the Senate;[5]—Col. L. J. Alston, Mr. (Gen.)
Blount (and his lady) of the House of R.[6]—Mons. Chevalier a
Fr. Gent. of Virg. and 2 lads are the boarders. No liquor is
provided but each one who wants applies to the landlord and
it is procured for him. Each boarder has a separate room furnished and a bell to call a servant when wanted; one can call
for a cold cut of victuals any time of day if wanted. After
dinner walked about 2 m. to the Rom. Catholic Coll. in George

[1] Annals of Congress, 1808–1809. pp. 788–806, report David R. Williams's speech.

[2] John Culpepper.

[3] Philip Barton Key.

[4] Thomas Newton, jr.

[5] Thomas Sumter of South Carolina, John Milledge of Georgia. Abram Trigg, member of Congress, not Senator, from Virginia.

[6] Lemuel J. Alston of South Carolina, Thomas Blount of North Carolina.

Town. There are 2 edifices—one is 3 stories high very long and spacious, with a chapel and about 3 or 4 School Rooms on the lower floor. On the 2nd floor an exhibition room in the middle and school rooms at each end. On the 3d floor is the Dormitory in the middle and rooms for the masters at each end. In the garrett is more room for a Dormitory if ever wanted. Mr. Boling one of the Prof⁵ a single man of about 26 or 30 took me into the different apartments and gave me considerable information about the Seminary. There is a President, who superintends the whole but does nothing in teaching. 4 Professors 1 of Poetry and Syntax, 1 of Grammar, who also teaches the Mathematics—1 of Rudiments and 1 of Elements. None are admitted younger than 8 nor older than 14. They remain till they have finished the course and often longer. Several of the students are over 20 and 22 who have been here ever since they were 14. The class of Elements consists of those boys who first begin the Latin tongue. The class of Rudiments read authors of some repute and have their character explained, and they learn to imitate their style.—They also learn Geography. The next pursues the Mathematics and learns more of the nature and true principles of grammar. The fourth becomes Rhetoricians. There is a Prof. of Divinity whose business it is, as far as I learned, to instruct in Divinity those older and more advanced students who wish to acquire Theological knowledge. They rise at 6 in the winter and while washing &c something is read from the "Spiritual Book." Then they are required to attend in the chapel where, all kneeling, prayers are said. At ¼ past 8 in the evening they attend evening service and at ½ past 8 all are required to retire to bed.—They all sleep in one room. The beds are all single, cot bedsteads the clothes all alike and like the curtains. There is a large frame like a single bed, divided into thirty snug apartments which are little alcoves with a curtain drawn before them. There are about 40 students—mostly professors of the Catholic religion. These are the proper Sons and favorites of the College, and are called Pensioners not because they are supported by the institution, for they are not;—they pay their own expenses. Protestant boys are admitted and a few of the present students are Protestants, but they do not sleep and eat with the Pensioners, but board out in town and are not intimately connected with the College. The Students all study in a room together under the constant inspection of a Professor. Mr.

B. took me to the room.—We stood at the door and all rose as we viewed them by candlelight. They always have an officer with them at recreation likewise. None are allowed even to walk out into town or any where else to trade or for any purpose without permission from the Principal, and if the Scholar is a young one he chooses some older, grave and experienced scholar for his companion and attendant, who goes with them to the shops and other places, as his guardian. The masters watch very vigilantly over the manners and morals of the youth; who rarely wish to act viciously, they being habituated to virtuous ways and influenced by the religious principles they profess. On Sunday they are required to attend service at the Church near by. They have one exhibition yearly, in August, which excites to much competition. The Coll. confers no degrees—Mr. B. did not seem to have accurate notions on the subject. The Seminary was founded on individuals' donations by a number of gentlemen associated for the purpose.— The Leg. have shown a willingness to patronize it on certain conditions relative to the unlimited admission of all Protestants, but the founders and friends thought it better to be independent and pursue their own way. The other building is 2 st. high square and appropriated to the instructors. It is common for a man on entering his son to signify to the President the sphere of life which he desires to move in, and then his course of education though not materially altered, has a turn given to it adapted to that sphere. The Pres. a worthy old man much beloved and respected yesterday died and is tomorrow to be buried.—Returned to my lodgings about 7 and went to bed. Expences today were Bill at the Ind. Queen, Alexa. for Horse at 3 qts grain &c. Lodg. and sling. 92—Martingale with steel hooks and buckles 1.50—Cake and gin .08—Hostler for cleaning bridle .08—Ferry at G. T. .12. Bounce and cake .09. = 2.80.

Sat. Dec. 10th. Weather a little warmer. Some rain in the Morn. Rose early and walked to G. T. market with Mr. O'Neal. Breakfasted on coffee, warm buckwheat cakes, chicken corncakes toast, broiled fresh pork &c. After breakfast set out for the Capitol with Mr. Chevalier and arrived before the H. of R. formed. About the time of proceeding to business, viz: eleven, Gen. Varnum the Speaker[1] rapped on the table and Mr. Brown a Baptist Clerg^n the Chaplain of the House went into the

[1] Joseph B. Varnum of Massachusetts.

Clerk's place fronting the Speaker's chair and addressed the throne of grace in a modest, appropriate, *republican* prayer of about 8 or 10 minutes, about half the members being in and observing great decorum and apparent seriousness. A few minutes after the Speaker took the chair of his own accord and looking round to see if a quorum were present, requested members to take their seats. No roll was called. The Cl. read over yesterday's proceedings and then the various business of the day was entered on; such as hearing reports of committees and presenting petitions—till at length the unfinished business of yesterday was introduced viz the resolution about Submission to the edicts of G. B. Mr. Cook of Mass.[1] a Rep. who voted for the embargo made a long, dry uninteresting speech of more than an hour; proposing some substitute for the embargo—A very handsome—neat, well-dressed man, but not a fluent speaker—tolerably good sense but no imagery. Nothing to embellish his Style and frequently ungrammatical. Mr. Jno. Randolph[2] made a few desultory remarks prefacing a motion of adjournment. I hardly ever in my life felt so interested in the speech of another, especially a speech of merely an accidental, careless nature. A person rose,—to appearances a boy of about 15 or 16—resembling in countenance young Martin of the S. C. College. A voice quite Shrill but very boyish and a look quite effeminate. I supposed it some newly elected and very young member who was not about to do much but observed that he rose and spoke with perfect composure and confidence. His figure and his voice much resembled those of my classmate Elliot. I asked who it was and was told J. Randolph. I was struck with astonishment. In one point of view I saw a tall slim boy who had all the time been sitting in a remote part of the house with his shoulders shrugged up and his light drab surtout closely buttoned up to his chin, a large pair of gloves or mittens on his hands, and his slim legs with white top boots thrown impolitely over the top of the next row of seats, as though he was a mere silent, indifferent spectator, or else perhaps too bashful to come forward in sight and take an active part. He got up and said he was fairly tired down with that discussion which had been so long protracted from day to day. Boldly and pointedly accused the Speaker of wandering from the subject. said the greatest part of the arguments had nothing to do with the sub-

---

[1] Orchard Cook.   [2] John Randolph of Roanoke.

ject, that the question of the merits of the Yazoo claim might with just as much propriety have been discussed as the merits of the Embargo, and as he did not wish the q. now taken because he knew of some members out of their seats who desired not to have it appear they were absent at the time, he would, though not in the habit of making that motion, now move for adjt.—In another point of view I saw a great Orator, Statesman, Scholar and man of genius, the first man in a great assembly of the Representatives of a great and free people—whose Sway has been extensive and whose influence is still considerable; whose fame is spread far and wide and sounded even beyond the Atlantic. These two impressions though apparently inconsistent, were made from the sight of the same man. His vote however was negatived by a small maj—Mr. Jackson[1] a republican merchant from R. Island read a speech of about ¾ hour setting forth the sufferings of the Eastern people and proposing to let the merchants arm vessels, and take off the Embargo. It was tolerably written for a mercantile character though it had a number of herebys, thereofs whereofs &c. and was read in a very clerical, drawling, monotonous tone,—*cleared* and all such words he would pronounce with the "ed" brought out full. The word "*it*" he would emphasize often at the end of sentences. In short he appeared like a very good respectable sensible man but not used to public life and habits of speaking. Age about 45 or 50, plain dark dress and good manners, modesty characterized him. Mr. Mumford[2] of the city of N. Y. replied to the remarks of an impudent young member from Vir. who had said the other day that the powdered headed gentry of the cities of the north might turn manufacturers and come round and take off the cotton of the South. Or even let them go to the plough—it would be no disgrace to them—they can be as respectable in that way as they can in commercial life." Mr. M. seemed hurt at the observation of Gholson and thought him lacking in a spirit of liberality, harmony and conciliation. Mr. Livermore of Mass. or N. H.[3] rose to Speak but a mot. for adjt was carried. Mr. Pitkin of Farmington[4] came into the gallery to see me, invited me to his lodgings at Mr. Frost's and also proposed to introduce me to the President on Monday. Mr. Taylor[5] of Columbia also came

---

[1] Richard Jackson.
[2] Gurdon S. Mumford.
[3] Edward St. Loe Livermore of Massachusetts.
[4] Timothy Pitkin. jr.
[5] John Taylor.

up, chatted awhile and invited me to his mess at Mrs. Hamilton's to see Mrs Taylor and Miss Goodwin. The House adjd at 3.—Walked home with Mr. O'Neal and at 4 sat down to dine in a goose, duck, chicken pye, Boiled corud beef, Roast fresh beef, hominy made of dry corn and beans boiled whole, sweet and Irish potatoes, custards, roast apples, crackers and butter with cheese preserves and cyder. Rose from table after sunset. Gen. Sumter is a still man at table—of genteel military manners, making now and then a very sensible remark. Gov. Milledge is more plain in dress and rude in manners. If a poor man and low station he might be thought ill mannerly. He took a piece of bread in his fingers, sopped in the gravy of the Roast Beef and ate it all at one mouthful though large enough for three. Afterwards there being a pretty large piece of quince on the plate of preserves and some sauce, he hauled the saucer near, took the quince in his thumb and finger and gormandized the whole at a bite. Gen. Trigg is more foppish in dress than any of them, powdered hair and silk stockings (or resembling them)—He talks some but less than Milledge, and not in so earnest, forward, dictatorial manner. Gen. Blount (pronounced Blunt) is a younger man—perhaps 35 or 40—pretty sensible and perspicuous and appropriate language—reads with much propriety, but is probably a violent partisan and strong in his prejudices. Col. Alston is full of polite airs and polite talk;—not a great man, but a pretty man. I once saw him in S. C. but did not now recognize him till I heard his name and he seems not to recollect me. Blount eulogized D. R. Williams speech and thought it transcendantly elegant. I was disposed to pay some respect to his judgment till being asked how Key spoke he said rather dull—for K in my estimation is the most musical, interesting, elegant Speaker that has risen. but Blount was led away by too much regard for the causes they severally espoused, and overlooked their eloquence abstractedly considered— Mr. Blount was in Cong. in Adams time when the direct tax was laid and said he voted for it expressly for the purpose of effecting a change of administration, knowing that the odium of the people could be awakened in no better way than by touching their interest. Mr. Milledge avowed the Same motive for his vote in that occasion saying that he knew it would lead the people to look into the causes of the measures and then they would perceive them built on false principles and having a wrong tendency. Gen. Trigg declared off and said he uniformly perseveringly voted against the direct tax and other odious measures because he thought them wrong. At 6 p. m. attended the Bap. Ch. with Mr. O'Neal and Mr. Scott (a religious young man of literature who is writing something on the Types) and heard a very handsome discourse delivered by Mr. Graham a young Bap. Clergyman lately arrived from Scotland.—A considerable audience. Many persons of both sexes and of very decent dress and demeanor seemed very devout. Singing rather boisterous and not well regulated. Returned and took supper with Mr. O'Neal and his family. An old lady or two his relations from N. Jersey were here and one of them seemingly a Methodist attacked O'Neal on his falling off—for Mr. O'N. was once an earnest apparently sincere professor of religion and still regards it, but does not, I suppose think himself religious and has contracted some singular notions about the Scriptures and Christianity. He approves the New Test't but disbelieves many facts stated in the old. Mr. O'N. Says there are as many as 15 churches within 4 or 5 miles of here. Mr. O'N. tells me he spent 3 m. in N. J. last summer to defeat Sloan's reelection and succeeded, as also another member's; because they were active in attempting to remove the seat of Gov. to Phil.—He says he used to be the most "populous" man in that county and had Still many connexions, much acquaintance and considerable influence.

Sun. Dec. 11th * * * After service Mr. P. took me into various parts of the Capitol and explained them. He says the wing which is devoted to the H. of R. cost upwards of 300,000 Dlls. and that it is said by persons who have an opportunity to know, that there is not in Europe a room equally superb with the Representatives Chamber. It is elliptical—Surrounded with 22 or 24 Corinthian Columns—Shaded on all sides with red flannel curtains. The light comes in at top through the Sky lights, the glass of which is an inch thick and cost several (perhaps 10) dollars a pane. The Speakers Chair is very superb and surrounded with the richest scarlet and green velvets and gold fringe. It resembles more the trappings of royalty than the seat of republicanism. The windows have all rich scarlet curtains of velvet with yellow gold fringe and gilt frames. Rich carpets of a Turkey kind cover the floors. The seats are all stuffed and adapted to ease, the tables for the members are elegant cabinet work. * * *

Mon. Dec. 12th. Weather quite mild and pleasant. After breakfast walked to Mr. Pitkin's lodgings at Frost's. Went with him to the Capitol where he introduced me to Mr. Davenport of Conn. and Mr. Holmes of Vir.[1] Chairman of the Com. of Claims. Visited the Library, large and well composed—perhaps 2000 volumes. Attended the Senate. Mr. Clinton,[2] their President has a most grave, dignified and venerable appearance. The Senate Room is smaller and much less superb than the Representatives. Gen. Smith of Baltimore spoke in a masterly, strong, forcible and perspicuous manner on post roads. Mr. Giles said a few words. Strength and perspicuity without much gracefulness. Mr. Pickering, a grave old man spoke briefly in proposing an amendment. Thence went round towards the Hall of the H. of R. and the doors being closed I stood out eating fruit near the Capitol among the people, when who should accost me but my old worthy friend and classmate Elihu Spencer, who told me he had lived in Mr. Gallatin's family 10 or 12 weeks. We walked to the Navy Yard saw the Naval Monument to the memory of the Heroes of Tripoli. Saw multitudes of Ball, Bombshells and Cannon, Ships, Stores, rigging &c. Returned and heard Mr. Gardenier[3] speak on the comparative merits of the past and present administration, with reference to the Embargo. He speaks very slowly but very correctly and has many nice and beautiful touches of painting in his oratory. He spoke very candidly, deliberately and interestingly. Dined on Goose, Fowl, Ham, Sausages and eggs &c. &c. Rode to George T. at Sunset. Returned Soon and spent the evening at my room with Mr. Spencer where we drank gin, ate apples and chatted most pleasantly until 9. At breakfast this morn the conversation happened to turn upon the employment of chaplains in Cong. Gen. Sumter and Gov. Milledge thought they had no business there. Gen. Blount and Gen. Trigg, thought it proper. Milledge said, in Monarchies such things were proper and consistent, but as we have determined that we have no church—no national religion, we ought not to have this semblance of it. Gen. Trigg said that true it is, we have no national church yet we have not discarded a God;—it is proper we have our

---

[1] John Davenport, jr.; David Holmes.

[2] George Clinton, Vice-President. The Senators whose names follow are Samuel Smith, William B. Giles of Virginia, Timothy Pickering of Massachusetts.

[3] Barent Gardenier, member of Congress from New York.

minds directed to him, and therefore public prayers by a clergyman is proper. Gen. S. asked if we could not direct our minds to God ourselves without the aid of a preacher. Prayers are no doubt proper in certain places—but in a political body they are quite out of place. Gen. T. said we should not many of us, for a week together think of God without the aid of a clergyman. Gen. Blount insisted on its happy influence and tendency and quoted one of the letters of Miranda's expedition to show the effect which public devotion had on even rough seamen when ordered by Capt. Lewis and how much they lost confidence in Miranda, because he did not attend the prayers.[1] Milledge said that was all owing to a principle of fear.

Tues. Dec. 13th. Cold, windy morn.—Wrote a letter to Mr. Chapman.—Breakfasted at the usual hour viz about 9 or ½ past and then walked to Mr. Smith's office [2] to turn the course of my papers to New Haven. Paid 3 Dolls in advance from Nov. 1, 1808 to Nov. 1, 1809. Smith is a sleek, nice little man of about 40. Somewhat bald. Windy weather, a little east of North.—About 12 o'c Mounted my horse and started. Called at Mr. Gallatin's about ½ hour to see Mr. Spencer. Drank some excellent *Liqueur* (a kind of cordial made in Philadelphia) saw Mr. G's likeness, chatted a while and rode on.

[1] See James Biggs's History of Don Francisco de Miranda's Expedition, Letter XIII, pp. 95, 96.

[2] Samuel H. Smith, editor of the National Intelligencer.

H. Doc. 353——59

www.ingramcontent.com/pod-product-compliance
Lightning Source LLC
Chambersburg PA
CBHW020041030726
47499CB00007B/2526